Married to the Man that Stole My Innocence

Nikki Rae

Married to the Man that Stole my Innocence

Copyright © 2020 by Nikki Rae

Published by Tyanna Presents

www.tyannapresents1@gmail.com

Synopsis

24-year old Nyla Thompson was raised in Camden, New Jersey, by both her parents along with her brother and sister. But after her parents tragically died in an accident when she was fifteen, it was left up to Nyla's older brother, Brandon, to pick up the pieces. He did the best he can, considering he was only nineteen himself. Raising two teenagers wasn't easy, but somehow Nyla manages to graduate high school and attend college. To celebrate, she goes on a trip that she'd dreamt about, along with her childhood best friend, Tasha. As the two of them plan to have the time of their life, things don't quite go the way they planned.

Zaire Price and his older brother Cameron has never been a statistic and either of them doesn't plan to start now. Doing whatever it took not to become a street boy, Zaire became a popular songwriter and producer. Though he's the celebrity, he becomes star-struck when he meets Nyla. There was no doubt in Zaire's mind that making

Nyla his woman would be a piece of cake. But he has no idea the barriers he's up against.

Will Zaire be able to use his charm to make the woman of his dreams his? Or will Nyla's past compromise her future of possibly being happy? Find out as you read this page-turner… Married to The Man That Stole My Innocence.

Chapter One

Nyla

"Bitch, are you good?" My best friend, Tasha, asked me because I was in a daze thinking about how my life was just starting to come together.

"Yeah, I'm good. I was just thinking about something, that's all. Anyway, what time are we going to the movies?" I asked.

"I was going to get tickets for the 6'oclock show. Are you good with that?"

"Yup, I'll be ready. Well, I'm about to be out. I have a few errands to run then you know I need to take a little nap."

"You need to go get yourself a man then maybe your life wouldn't be so damn boring," she shot back.

"My life is just fine," I told her, before heading out the door.

My name is Nyla Thompson. I was born and raised in Camden, NJ. I'm 24 years old, and I'm a social worker for the Board of Social Service on Market street. I have one brother and a sister and I'm the youngest. The three of us are very close. My parents died in a plane crash when I was just fifteen years old. So, my brother was forced to take care of me and my sister, Ariel, when my parents died since he was nineteen years and the oldest. He became a father figure to us. When it came to me and my sister, my brother Brandon didn't play. He wasn't a street dude or anything, but he was missing a few screws and would kill over his family and respect.

Ariel was only a year older than me, so we pretty much did everything together. My sister and Tasha were the only two females that I really fucked with because I didn't have time for the messy bullshit that I saw other females doing. After stopping past Price Rite and doing a little food shopping, I ran to Walmart for some cleaning supplies and some personals. After paying for my things, I pulled up to my one-bedroom apartment in the newly remodeled Shelton Terrace apartments in Centerville.

Once I got in the house, I put my groceries up then laid on the couch. I didn't even bother to turn the tv on because I knew I was going to fall asleep as soon as I got comfortable. I dozed off quickly just like I expected to.

"Please don't do this to me! Please stop!"

"Shut the fuck up and take this dick. You know you want it."

I jumped up out of my sleep sweating. I hated when I dreamed about my attack. That night was the worst night of my life. I've been dreaming about it since the night it happened and that was seven years ago. But it is something that will forever be embedded in my head. I walked into the bathroom and splashed some water on my face. I thought about making an appointment to see a therapist. I started seeing one when it first happened, but I stopped going because I didn't feel like it was beneficial to me.

I grabbed my phone and put it on the charger then walked in my room to see what I wanted to wear to the movies tonight. I decided on a pair of blue jeans, a black sweater, and my black thigh-high boots with the heel. I showered and then threw my clothes on, wearing my hair in a French braid. I grabbed my phone from the charger, placed it in my bag and headed out the door. After checking on my surroundings, I got in the car and headed to the movie theater. It took damn near a half hour to get there with this Saturday night traffic. When I got to the movies, I called Tasha but hung up when she walked over to the car. We were standing at the concession stand when I felt someone staring at me. When I turned around to check my surroundings, there was three dudes in the line next to ours. One guy, in particular, was staring at me and when he noticed that I was looking at him, he smiled and waved at me. I waved back but prayed he didn't try to talk to me.

We got our popcorn and drinks and headed to our seats. We were about to see Bad Boys For Life, featuring Martin Lawrence and Will Smith.

Three hours later, the movie was finally over, and Tasha and I decided to go to Applebee's, since it was right next door to the theater. It was after nine so happy hour was on and popping. I was going to order one drink and nothing more since I had to drive. I was more excited about the half off appetizers than I was about the drinks.

As we were walking over, I saw the same guys that was staring in the movie theater walking over to Applebee's as well.

"Did you ladies enjoy the movies?" I heard one of the guys say.

"Actually, I did. I love all the Bad Boy movies. Did you enjoy it?" I asked.

"Hell yeah, Bad Boys is that work," the one that was eye-fucking me, stated.

"Well, you guys enjoy the rest of your night," I replied while walking into Applebee's.

"You do the same, Chocolate Drop."

"Welcome to Applebee's. My name is Jenny and I'll be your waiter for the night. May I start you off with something to drink?"

"Yes, I'll have the strawberry martini please," I told her.

"And I'll have the same," Tasha chimed in.

"Okay. Do you need a minute to look over the menu or are you already to order?" The waiter asked.

"By the time you come back with the drinks, we'll be ready to order," I answered. When she came back with our drink orders, we ordered our appetizers and food. I looked over at the bar and noticed the guys from the movie theater. The one that has been staring waved at me and I waved back.

"Bitch, who the hell are you waving at?" I was about to show her, but when I looked up, he was walking to our table.

"Hello, beautiful. I'm Zaire and you are?" The nice-looking guy asked, holding his hand out for me to shake.

"Hi, Zaire. I'm Nyla," I told him. He kissed the back of my hand, and for some reason, it made me feel tingly and warm.

"Well, it's a pleasure to meet you, Nyla. I was wondering would it be too much to ask you out on a date?"

"Honestly, I'm not looking to date anyone at the moment," I told him, and Tasha nudged my arm.

"What she meant to say was leave your number, and she will hit you up when she's ready," Tasha stuck her nose in a place where it didn't belong, I just smiled.

"That's sounds good too. What's your name, pretty lady?" Zaire asked Tasha. She started cheesing from ear to ear.

"Tasha," she replied. I know this is going to sound crazy, but hearing him call her pretty lady made me feel some type of way. Not that Tasha wasn't pretty because she was that and more. I guess I was enjoying the attention that he was giving me, and I didn't want to share it with anyone else.

"I think my brother would like you. He's right over there if you would like to meet him," he stated while pointing over at the bar.

"I don't see any harm in meeting someone new," she told him with a smile as big as they come. He waved his brother to come over to the table, and he walked over to our table and introduced himself. Of course, Tasha had to be the one that invited them to join us, and of course, they didn't decline the offer. I looked over at the bar and didn't see the other guy that they were with at the movies.

We all ate and talked, and I was actually having fun and enjoying both of the guys' company. We finally decided to leave, and Zaire walked me to my car. I decided to go head and give him my number. He waited for me to get in my car and pulled off. As soon as I got in the house, I took my shower and laid across my bed, replaying my night out with Tasha, Zaire, and his brother Cameron. The thought of Zaire caused me to smile. My phone buzzing broke me from my thoughts. I looked at my phone and speak of the devil.

Zaire: Hey, Beautiful, it's Zaire. I just wanted to make sure that you made it home safely.

Me: Yes, I made it home safely. Thanks for checking on me.

Zaire: No problem, beautiful. You should let me take you out on a real date with just you and me. I can tell that you're feeling me, and you already know that I'm feeling you, so I don't see why we can't hang out and get to know one another.

I thought about what he said before responding and he was right.

Me: You're right; nothing is wrong with getting to know one another. So, I'll give you one date then we'll go from there.

Zaire: That's all I needed to hear. Well, get some rest, and I'll call you later on in the day. A nigga is beat and ready to get naked and take my ass to sleep. Good night, Beautiful.

Me: Good night, Zaire.

I plugged my phone up then drifted off to sleep, hoping like hell I didn't have another nightmare about my attack. But that was just wishful thinking because I tossed and turned all night long thinking about that horrible night. I knew I needed to see a therapist asap. I also knew that meant that I would have to relive every detail about that night, and I just didn't feel like I was ready for that right now. I wanted to talk to my brother and sister about it, but I knew they would make me go see someone immediately.

I looked up at the clock on my nightstand, and it was six in the morning, I threw a pillow over my face and tried to sleep again. I was ready to get a roommate just to see if the nightmares would stop. After tossing and turning for another half hour, I was out like a baby.

"Nyla, wake up." I heard a voice say in my sleep. I thought I was dreaming until I felt someone shaking me. I jumped up in a panic.

"What the hell is wrong with you?" My sister, Ariel, asked.

"You just startled me, that's all."

"Well, had you answered the door, I wouldn't had to use my key. And did you forget we're supposed to be having lunch with Brandon in less than an hour?"

"Oh shit, I totally forgot about that. Just give me a few minutes, I'll be ready." I jumped up and handled my hygiene. I didn't feel like getting dressed, so I threw on a pair of jeans, a shirt, and a pair of boots. It was the middle of fall, so my outfit was perfect. I put my hair in a messy bun then we headed out the door. I rode in Ariel's car because I didn't feel like driving. We pulled up at

Brandon's house, which was in Pennsauken, about twenty minutes from where I lived.

When I walked into my brothers' house, the aroma from the food caused my stomach to growl. I walked into the kitchen and my brother was setting our plates on the table.

"Hey, bro. This food smelling good."

"What's up, baby sis? You already know how I get down in the kitchen. I made some grilled barbeque salmon, red roasted potatoes, and sautéed asparagus."

"Damn, bro. What's the occasion?" Ariel chimed in.

"I'm glad you asked. Have a seat so we can eat and chat." We sat down, he blessed the food and I didn't waste any time digging in. Brandon could cook his ass off.

"So, I just wanted to let you guys know that your bro is about to be a daddy. Mariah is five months pregnant with my son, so y'all know a nigga happy as hell. I didn't tell y'all sooner because in the beginning she was having complications and I didn't want to get everybody hopes up. But the doctor cleared everything yesterday. So, I figured this was the perfect time to share with my two favorite ladies."

"Oh my God, bro! Congrats! I can't wait to spoil my nephew," I told him with a mouth full of food.

"Thanks, baby sis. I can't wait to meet my little man. I'm going to have him spoiled as shit." After Ariel and I congratulated him, we ate our food and talked bullshit as we normally did when we're all together.

"So, Nyla, what's been going on with you? It seems like I haven't spoken to you in about a week."

"Honestly, nothing except the nightmares that I keep having about my attack that night," I said lowly. The room fell silent until Brandon spoke again.

"See, this is why I told you that you needed to go to therapy. Nyla, you're not leaving here until you make an appointment to see someone. I know what happen to you was a tragedy, but that was damn near seven years ago, and it's still holding you back from living your best life. I really want you to live the greatest life that you can. Get married and have some kids, but how are you going to do that if you won't even go on a date with a man? You can't even sleep in peace because of what that bastard did to you." The tears fell freely down my face as I thought about everything that my brother was saying. I knew more than anyone that I needed to talk to someone, but I also knew that I would have to relive the entire night.

"Stop crying, sis. I can go with you if you want me to. But Brandon is right, your attack has way too much power over your life. You deserve nothing but the best and believe me when I tell you, this that piece of shit will get what's coming to him. God will never allow him to get away with that," Ariel assured me with tears in her eyes.

After I got myself together, we searched online for a therapist until one caught my eye. I dialed the number and made an appointment for next week. I actually felt good about the situation and couldn't wait to get it over with. We sat at my brother's house for about another hour before deciding to leave. When I got back home, I decided to take a nap since I barely got any sleep last night. As I was dozing off, I couldn't help but think about Zaire. So, when I woke up, I planned to give him a call and see what he was up to.

Chapter Two

Zaire

"Yo, you need to get the fuck off of my mom like that before I put a hot one in your chest!" I heard my brother, Cameron yelling as we were headed up to my mom's apartment. When me and my cousin got in the door, my brother was pointing a gun at some nigga's dome, while my mom stood there looking scared and high.

"What the fuck is going on in here?" I shouted.

"This bitch owes me money, and I'm not leaving until I get my shit, that's what's going on," the dude blurted. At that point, I knew this shit was about to go left. Cameron hit that nigga with the butt of the gun, and that nigga started leaking.

"Watch what the fuck you call my momma!" my brother yelled.

"Oh my God! Please stop!" My mom yelled. "I owe him two hundred dollars and he just want his money. Don't hurt him; he has the best drugs out here. He just wants his money. He would never hurt me."

Hearing my mom beg us to spare a nigga life that put his hands on her because he has good drugs broke my fucking heart. I damn near shed a tear over that shit.

"Yo, leave that nigga alone. If she owes him money, he needs to be paid," I told my brother.

"But I don't care what she owes you, don't ever lay a hand on my momma again or I'll end your life right where you stand," I warned that nigga. "Go in the bathroom and clean yourself up then let me holla at you for a minute," I told the dude. He walked in the bathroom, watching his back as he walked. Cameron and Brian were grilling the fuck out of him, waiting for him to make a wrong move.

When dude came back from the bathroom, I took him in the hallway to speak to him in private. I needed to know a few things about how far gone my momma was out in these streets. Once he told me that my mom be fucking and sucking for drugs, I knew I couldn't allow that. I also knew that the only way to stop her from doing that shit was to pay for it.

"Look, this is between you and me. I'm going to pay her debt, but I'm also going to give you money weekly for her needs. She's to only buy from you, and I swear you better not try to get the fuck over on her or me. How much do she usually spend a week on this shit y'all sell?"

"She usually comes to me about three times a day; sometimes it's only one if she's has all the money at one time. But she gets two bags every time she comes, so she usually spends 30 dollars a day on nicks, but if it's a good day, she spends 60 a day. She gets drugs every day of the week except Sunday. For some reason, she won't get high on that day."

"Aight, cool. I'm going to give you your money that she owes you plus an extra thousand to last for a month. I come check on my mom two to three times a week, but I would really appreciate if you looked out for my mom's when I'm not around. I know she do what she does, but I don't want anything to happen to her. I love my momma to death and would hate for anything to happen to her. Just don't tell her that I'm the one paying for it, but from here on out, don't take any more of my moms' money." He just nodded in agreement and I gave him my burner cell number to contact me if he needed to.

I walked back into the house with my family. I know y'all probably think I'm crazy for paying for my mom's habit, but I don't think I am. I rather pay for it then having her life taken over a few hundred dollars. And it's not like she was going to stop just because we wanted her to. She had to want that shit for herself.

"Where that fuck boy at?" My brother asked.

"I sent his ass on his way," I replied, not really in the mood to answer any more questions.

I walked over and hugged my mom tightly. In that brief moment, I wondered how the hell did she start getting high? My mom had a decent office job at one point. I just hoped that she got her shit together sooner than later. We stayed there for about another hour or so before we decided to hit up the movies then happy hour. When I saw baby girl at the movies, I knew I wanted to talk to her. She was a beautiful chocolate drop with a banging ass body. Baby girl was thicker than a Snicker with a fat ass. The girl that she was with was a cutie too, but she didn't have anything on my chocolate drop. I watched her and her friend go into Applebee's, so I decided that's where my brother, my cousin, and myself would be headed. Because I refused to let the night go by without getting her number.

It was much harder to get her number than I thought it would be, and if it weren't for her friend, I probably wouldn't have got it. That would have been a first because I could have any woman I wanted, and I mean that literally. Getting pussy and women was never a problem for me. I had just left the gym with my brother when my phone buzzed indicating that I had a text message. I looked down at my phone and started smiling hard as hell.

Chocolate Drop: Good evening, Zaire, it's Nyla. I was just texting to see what you were up to.

Me: Good evening, Chocolate Drop. I'm just leaving the gym. What you up to? Are you trying to see me tonight? I asked, getting straight to the point.

Chocolate Drop: My name is Nyla, not chocolate drop. And if you weren't busy, I thought maybe we could get *something to eat and get to know one another, just the two of us.* That was all a nigga needed to hear.

Me: I'm sorry if I offended you by calling you chocolate drop, but I think that names suit you perfectly. You're more beautiful than any woman I've ever seen in my life. Your chocolate complexion is beyond beautiful. And as far as getting something to eat, I'm down. Just give me about an hour to shower and throw some clothes on then I'll come pick you up. Just shoot me your address.

Chocolate Drop: I'm not offended and okay. I'll be ready when you get here. Shooting you my address now.

Nothing else was said. I was driving home from the gym happier than a gay man in a faggot camp. I pulled up to my house and in less than ten minutes so I could get dressed.

Let me introduce myself properly. My name is Zaire Price, and I'm 27 years old. I was born and raised in South Philadelphia. I have my own recording label, and I'm one of the biggest record producers in the world. My name rings bells all over the world. I wasn't into the streets, but there wasn't an ounce of pussy in me. I could be calm, cool, and collective, but I would turn into something vicious if I was fucked with. I had no problem with putting a bullet in a nigga if I had to. It was just me and my older brother, Cameron. My mom let the hard streets of Philly take over her life. She let drugs cause her to lose everything that she worked so hard to get. I loved my mom with everything in me, but she wasn't ready to get herself together, and I had to respect that. But no matter what, I'll always be there for her. I didn't agree with her habit, but I'll always make sure she's straight. Me and my brother were damn near one in the same. The only difference between the two of us was he would kill your ass for a lot less than I would. He's always been the angry one coming up. And the fact that we didn't know who our father was didn't make it any better. We were both determined to be somebody important in the world. We refused to become a part of the world's statistics. So, we did what we had to do. We both graduated high school and got our college degrees with the help of my Aunt Pat and her husband, Uncle Brad. My aunt Pat was my mom's sister and my cousin Brian's mom. Brian was like a brother to us since we were raised together.

I was now dressed and ready to take my chocolate drop out. I got to her house in about twenty minutes. I knocked on the door, and when she opened the door, my words got caught in my throat. That's how beautiful she looked. She had on all black with red accessories and some red boots and a red leather coat. Her hair was bone straight. It was pretty long, so I wasn't sure if it was her hair or not, but as good as she looked, I didn't give a damn if it was a wig that she borrowed from a friend.

"You look stunning, chocolate drop."

"Thanks, Zaire. You're looking pretty handsome yourself," she replied.

She locked up her apartment and we headed to the car. I opened the door for her and waited for her to get inside. In less than thirty minutes later, I pulled up at Warm Daddy's. I figured we could eat some good ass soul food and listen to some live music. This was one of my favorite places; the music was relaxing, and the food was good as hell. I opened her car door, grabbed her hand, headed to the entrance. Once we were in and seated, our waiter came over and took our drink orders.

"I've always wanted to come here but never got around to it," Nyla stated.

"Well, I'm glad that I could be the one to bring you. This is a really nice and low-key spot. I think you'll like it and the food is good too," I told her. The waiter came back and took our order, we talked and got to know one another while we waited.

"So, what do you do for a living?" Nyla asked.

"I'm a record producer. I have my own record label over here in Philly," I told her.

"Oh wow, I would have never guessed. So, are you telling me that I'm on a date with a famous man?" She asked playfully.

"I'll just say that I'm a big deal and work with a lot of famous people."

"How famous are we talking? These little new boys that's out like, Lil Uzi and Designer?" She asked with a giggle.

"*I see you have jokes. Hell no, I wouldn't put my name on no shit those niggas rapping about. But to answer your question, I'm talking Beyoncé famous,*" *I replied. She spat her drink out at my response and I just smiled. "Now let's talk about you. What do you do for a living?"*

"*I'm a social worker for the Board of Social Service.*"

"*That's wassup. So, is that your dream job or is it just something to do for now?*" *I asked.*

"*Honestly, I'm working on opening up my own mentoring company for teens and young adults that have been sexually assaulted,*" *she stated lowly.*

"*I think that's dope. If there's anything that I could do to help, please let me know. I mean, anything, including money. You won't owe me anything because I'll be doing it for a good cause and giving back,*" *I told her honestly. She stared at me for a few seconds before responding. I think she was trying to figure out if I was serious or not.*

"*Thanks, I really appreciate the offer. I may even take you up on it, but let's discuss that at another time.*"

"Okay, cool, but I do have one more question. Why do you want to mentor rape victims?" She was quiet and looked caught off guard by my question.

"Because someone really important to me was raped, and I figured I should do something positive and give back to my community at the same time. My friend still has a very difficult time dealing with her rape," she replied sadly. I just nodded in agreement.

I decided to leave the topic alone for now. To be honest, that shit hit a soft spot. I think what she's trying to do would be great, and if I help her out with this project, it would help clear my conscience from some of the things that I did that I'm not proud of.

"So, tell me about your family. Do you have siblings and are your parents still together?" I bombarded her with questions.

"Actually, my parents died in a plane crash, so my brother raised me and my older sister. But before they died, they were the best parents that you could ask for. How about you?"

"I have one brother and I have no clue who my father is. As far as my mom goes, she let the streets get a hold to her. I've tried to help her numerous times, but she won't give up the drugs," I told her sadly. I was surprised that I was that comfortable telling her all of that.

"I'm sorry, I didn't mean to pry."

"You're not prying, but I would like to change the subject and get to know you a little better." She just politely smiled. We sat for the next hour talking and chilling. I was really feeling her vibe, but I can also tell that she wasn't used to the dating shit either. The truth was neither was I. I mean, I fucked around with chicks all the time. I even took a few women out to dinner a time or two, but it was nothing major. It was something about Nyla that made me want to get to know her. She actually reminded me of someone, I just couldn't figure out who it was.

I dropped her back off at home, and once she was in the house, I took my ass home. I pulled up to my driveway and something seemed off. I took my gun from under the seat and walked into my home with caution. When I walked in, my shit had been ransacked. I cursed myself for not putting my alarm on. I guess I was too in a rush to pick up Nyla to remember. I heard a noise upstairs, and as I was creeping up the steps and the nigga was coming out of my guest bedroom, but he wasn't carrying anything. I popped that nigga right in the chest, not caring if he lived or died.

"Why the fuck is you in my house, nigga?" I asked, standing over top of him, pointing a gun at his dumb ass as he bled on my damn carpet.

"You weren't supposed to be here," he managed to say before coughing up blood.

"What the fuck you mean I wasn't supposed to be here? Nigga, did somebody send you to my house?" But that nigga died right there on my floor. I called the cops then Cameron, who answered on the second ring.

"Yo, bro, wassup?"

"Yo, I need you to come to the house asap. I just killed somebody," I told him.

"Nigga, what the fuck! Are you serious?"

"Hell yeah, I'm serious. Somebody broke in my fucking house, just get here," I told him. I heard my doorbell, and when I got down there, it was the cops. I let them in and told them what happened. I wasn't worried about being charged because my gun was legal, and that nigga was in my home.

They walked upstairs to get the body, and the officer that I was talking to was writing down what I was saying. A couple minutes later, I heard my brother downstairs talking shit because the officers wouldn't let him come upstairs to the crime scene. We walked downstairs so the ambulance could bring the body out. Cameron and my cousin Brian were both downstairs. By now all my nosey ass neighbors were outside. Once the body was out the house, we all rode to the police station together, but something wasn't right. I could feel it deep down. All I kept replaying was him saying you weren't supposed to be here.

✯✯✯✯✯

It's been two weeks since that shit went down and I still had no idea why that nigga was at my house. I had just got to Camden. I was on my way to Nyla's job to take her some lunch. I was really feeling Nyla. Her and I saw one another every day and talked several times a day. I could tell that she was battling some shit, but I didn't want to pry, I figured when she was comfortable enough to tell me, she would. When I got to Nyla's job, I texted her that I was in the lobby. Nyla walked out smiling, but I could tell that she had some deep shit going on in her head. I decided not to bother asking what was wrong because she always said nothing, yet I would always catch her daydreaming.

"Zaire, thank you so much for lunch," she said sweetly

"Anything for you. Well, I can't stay long, but I'll love to see you tonight if it's possible?"

"Sure, I don't have anything planned," Nyla answered. After we shared a hug, I headed back over Philly, because I had some shit to handle at the studio.

I was at the studio going over some music when my assistant Sharee walked into my office, closing the door behind her. I could tell by the look in her eyes that she was coming in here for some dick, but I wasn't trying to go there with her ass. I thought I made that clear the last time she tried that shit.

"Hey, Zaire. Wassup with you?" Sharee asked, walking towards me.

"Shit, trying to get some work done. Wassup with you?"

"Not much I came in here to see if you were still on that bullshit you were talking last week about us not fucking anymore?" I just shook my head because it was hard as hell for me not to bend Sharee's ass over and fuck her on my desk. Sharee had some good pussy, but I was really trying to see what was up with me and Nyla. I knew if I wanted something different with Nyla, then I was gonna have to do something different.

"Look, Sharee, I meant what I said last week. I can't fuck with you like that. Just chill. We can still be cool; we just can't do anything sexual. Besides, don't you think it's time that you do right by your nigga?" Sharee looked at me with a scowl on her face that let me know she wasn't too happy with what I just said.

"You got some fucking nerve, Zaire. Now you worried about me having a boyfriend. Y'all niggas ain't shit. I swear y'all ain't!" she yelled.

"I think you need to watch who the fuck you talking to like that and get out of my office before you say some shit that will leave you jobless," I told her. I didn't do well with disrespect and Sharee was out of pocket all because I didn't want to fuck her anymore.

"Man, fuck you, Zaire," she yelled loudly before storming out of my office. I swear I wanted to choke the fuck out of her little ass. Shit like that was the reason why I hated fucking these bitches because they acted fucking crazy. I mean, yeah, I enjoyed fucking her, but it was never that deep. I damn sure never took her seriously 'cause she had a man. I thought she was just fucking me because she had a fuck boy on her hands.

"Yo, what the fuck your girl out there tripping about?" My brother asked, walking into my office. "She out there popping shit bout something all loud and got everybody looking at her like she's crazy."

"She just mad because I told her I wasn't fucking her anymore and told her to work shit out with her nigga."

"Damn, nigga. I told your ass to stop giving these bitches that crack dick. You know that shit be having those bitches strung out," Cameron chuckled at his own comment. My brother was right; the dick be having bitches straight bugging out.

"Anyway, what brings you by?" I asked.

"I think I have an idea who sent that nigga to your house, but we need to do our homework first before we murk him," Cameron said seriously. Cameron now had my undivided attention.

"I think it was that nigga Mike. From what I heard, the nigga you killed was his cousin, so I know that shit wasn't no coincidence."

I could feel my face turning red. Mike was a nigga from another record label. See, Mike wasn't nowhere near as big as I was in the music business, and I could tell that he was one of those jealous niggas. But what I'm not getting is what was the purpose of breaking in my house. I need to know what he was looking for because the guy made it clear that I wasn't supposed to be there. Which made me wonder how the hell did he know I wouldn't be home? Listening to Cameron really had my head spinning. I wanted answers and I was about to go get them. I jumped up from my seat ready to go see Mike. I grabbed my belongings, ready to head out, but Cameron stopped me.

"Chill, we need to do our homework first, so when we go see that nigga, we'll know for sure what's up. I'm working on something now. But anyway, are you still talking to the girl from Applebee's?" Camron asked.

"Hell yeah, I ain't trying to fuck that up. I'm actually feeling her chocolate ass," I told him.

"I know you hit that already, didn't you?"

"Nah, we just be chilling. We haven't even talked about sex yet to be honest."

"Shid, your ass is slipping, bro. I'm still talking to her best friend, and I done hit that shit a few times already. Her homegirl is cool, and she definitely got some bomb ass pussy, but you know I'm not settling down with no chick," Cameron stated, serious as hell. My brother always said it was too much pussy in the streets to be tied down to one chick. "We are going out tonight for some wings at Romans, if you and your people's want to tag along."

"Aight, I'll hit her up and see what's up, then I'll let you know," I told Cameron.

Camron left, and I just chuckled to myself because my brother must be feeling Nyla's friend if they're going out together. The fact that he said he already hit it about three times within the last couple of weeks told me a lot because Cameron don't take chicks out. He only fucks the same girl four times total to prevent himself from catching feelings.

I had a new artist coming in today, so I was about to go sit in on his session to check him out. When I walked out of my office, Sharee looked at me and rolled her eyes. I just chuckled to myself and kept walking. I made it to the studio where the new artist was located, and I had to admit he was pretty dope. He had that Tyrese voice when Tyrese first came out. I listened to the entire song and I knew he was gonna make him and I tons of money. Once he was done, him and I talked for a little. I offered him a contract immediately, but I told him to make sure that he goes over it with a lawyer. When he was ready, I wanted him and his lawyer to meet with me and my company lawyer.

★★★★★

Later that evening, I picked Nyla sexy ass up and met up with my brother and her homegirl. When I pulled up, the parking lot was damn near full. We walked in, I found my brother and walked over to the table. After pulling out Nyla's chair and waited for her to be seated, I took my seat. We ordered some drinks and then looked at the menu. We all decided to just order different types of flavored wings. This chick was up on the mic singing Karaoke sounding a hot damn mess. We all laughed amongst ourselves at the girl, but that was the good thing about karaoke. You didn't have to know how to sing because it was meant to be fun.

"Nyla, we should go up and do Karaoke. We both know how to sing better than that," Tasha said to Nyla.

Now that should be interesting watching them do Karaoke, I thought.

"You can take your ass up there, but you know I'm not doing Karaoke," Nyla replied.

"You're so corny," Tasha said to Nyla while playfully mugging her. "Fine, I'll go up there by myself. I'm about to go sign up," Tasha replied while getting up from the table.

"What are you going to sing?" Cameron asked as soon as Tasha got back to the table.

"You'll see in a few minutes. I have one other person a headed of me," she replied with a big smile. My brother smiled hard at her, and I could tell by the way he looked at her that he was feeling her. I actually liked her for him. Tasha seemed to have a freer and more open spirit than Nyla. Nyla was fun, but she was more on the laid-back side. The DJ called Tasha to the front, and Nyla grabbed her cell to record and Cameron did the same thing. I just smirked and popped another garlic parmesan wing into my mouth. The instrumental to **"If I ain't got you"** by Alicia Keys started playing. As soon as Tasha opened her mouth, I damn near choked on my chicken, that's how blown away I was by her voice. Tasha took that song to another level. Her voice was unique. Of course, she would need some help to make it big, and that's where I come in at.

"Yo, your girl can sing her ass off. Why you didn't tell me she could blow like that?" I asked Nyla.

"Honestly, I didn't know she could blow like that either. I mean, I knew she had a nice little tune, but she ain't never sing like that around me before," Nyla stated.

"Damn, she just made my dick hard," Cameron blurted out of nowhere. All I could do was chuckle at his comment. When she finished the song, everyone clapped and cheered for Tasha. Tasha sashayed back over to the table, smiling hard as hell and Cameron starting loudly clapping like a proud boyfriend.

"Tasha, your voice is amazing. I could really take you to the top with that voice," I told her honestly.

"Thanks, Zaire, but you don't have to gas me up because you are fucking with my friend," Tasha replied.

"Nah, I'm dead ass. No pressure tonight, but when you get a minute, you and Nyla need to drop by the label. I'm gonna put you in a booth," I told Tasha seriously.

"You dead ass?" she asked.

"I'm dead ass, Tasha." She was excited as hell. I couldn't lie; I was happy too. I couldn't wait to get her in a studio.

For the rest of the night, we just chilled and got acquainted with one another. You could tell that Nyla and Tasha was super tight. They acted more like sisters than they did best friends.

After we left, I dropped Nyla back off at her place. I lowkey wanted her to invite me in because I didn't want the night to end just yet, but I didn't want to come off as being thirsty. But that didn't happen. I walked Nyla to her door and hugged her goodbye. I tried my luck and leaned in for a kiss, and surprisingly, she let me. The minute she started kissing me back, I wish I didn't kiss her because my dick was brick hard. I was ready to fuck right then and there. I broke the kiss before shit got out of hand.

"I had a great time with you tonight, Nyla. I would really love to continue this and see where things can go," I told Nyla honestly.

"I really had a nice time with you too, Zaire," Nyla stated.

"That's good to know. Well, I'm gonna set up something special for just the two of us," I told her, and she just smiled at me. I had to go because her chocolate ass had a nigga dick hurting from being so hard.

We said our final goodbyes, and then I jumped in my car and peeled off. Chocolate Drop had me ready to fuck something. Typically, I would have been balls deep in Sharee, but I ain't fucking that crazy bitch no more. I guess I had to go home and beat my dick. I didn't feel like fucking around with these thirsty hoes tonight, so I took my black ass home.

Chapter Three

Cameron

"Ah shit! Tasha, this pussy feels good as shit!" I groaned while I was deep stroking Tasha's tight, super wet pussy. I had Tasha in doggy style, hitting that shit. Her pussy was so fucking good I was trying not to cum quick. I didn't want her to think I was a minute man because I was far from it. The one thing I knew for sure was that I could deliver some great dick. But shorty was about to make me sound like a liar the way she was throwing that good pussy back.

"Oh fuck! Cameron, fuck me harder!" Tasha moaned, and her wish was my command. I sped up my strokes and prayed that she was about to cum because I damn sure was about to, and I didn't want to get mine before she got hers. I slapped Tasha on the ass.

"Cum for me, ma. Cum all over this dick," I groaned while beating that pussy up.

"Fuck, Cameron! I'm about to cum all over this big dick!" Tasha yelled.

"Fuck, ma! I'm about to cum too!" I groaned loudly before I shot my load in the condom then collapsed on the bed. I needed to recuperate, but once I was done, I knew I was getting some more of that good-good. I just hoped she was ready for countless nuts and a lack of sleep.

After fucking for hours, we were both worn out. Shorty wasn't no amateur to this fucking thing. Tasha could ride it dick like it was going out of style. Before I knew it, we had both fell into a deep sleep.

★★★★★

When I woke up, the sun was shining in my face. I looked over and Tasha was still sleeping peacefully. I grabbed my phone off the nightstand to look at the time. It was damn near noon. I haven't slept that long in a minute, that's how I knew shit was real last night. I got up to use the bathroom and handle my hygiene. Out of nowhere, my stomach started growling loud as hell.

I didn't really want to fuck with Tasha's sleep, but a nigga was hungry, and I wanted to see if she wanted to grab some lunch. When I got back to the room, Tasha was already awake, but she was still laying down.

"Good afternoon, beautiful."

"Afternoon? What time is it?" Tasha asked while grabbing for her phone. "Damn, that was some good sleep."

"That's what happens when a nigga put that good dick up in you," I told her. Tasha blushed before replying.

"So, I guess that means I put the good pussy on you because I know that you just woke up also," Tasha shot back. All I could do was laugh and shake my head. Tasha was so outgoing and funny.

"Yeah, I guess you can say that. Listen, a nigga is starving. You want to go get something to eat? I think I want some Cajun chicken and shrimp pasta from Friday's," I told her.

"Hell yeah, I'm starving, and I love that pasta, but I need you to take me pass my house so I can wash my ass and put some clean clothes on."

"Aight, bet and don't be taking all long because I'm starving," I said to Tasha, jokingly.

"Don't worry, I won't, but always remember you can't rush perfection," she replied with a big grin.

It's only been a couple of weeks since I met Tasha, but I had to admit I was kinda feeling her. Tasha's personality was big and vibrant, not to mention she was beautiful with a banging ass body. When we got to Tasha's apartment, I was amazed at how nice it was on the inside for a Camden Apartment. Hell, some would say it was better than my three-bedroom house I lived in located in Woodbury, New Jersey as far as the décor.

"Damn Tash, this is really nice. Did you decorate this yourself?"

"Thanks, but nope. This is all the work of Nyla. She lives for this type of stuff. I don't have the patience or the eye. I told her she needs to open up her own business doing decorating and event planning," Tasha said. I knew then I was about to get Nyla to come redo my company over, especially my office.

"This is dope. I need her to do some work for me and I'll make sure it's worth her time."

"Cool, she'll love that," Tasha yelled from the shower. I helped myself to the rest of the house, becoming even more intrigued but Nyla's work. Once I was finished touring the apartment, I sat down in the living room, checking my social media while I waited for Tasha to come out.

The name is Cameron Price, and I'm twenty-nine years old. I'm just a year older than my baby brother, Zaire. I was born and raised in South Philly. I started my own accounting company three years ago, and everything was going good so far. I had two houses; one in my hometown and one in Woodbury, New Jersey, which is the house I stay at most nights since Woodbury is where my company is located. Not knowing who my father was and having a mother that was on drugs only made me and my brother more determined to make it in the world. Not become a statistic of what people expect from us blacks whose parents are on drugs. So, I made a vow to make sure that me or my brother made something positive out our lives, and we both did.

I couldn't have been proud of myself and my brother. He had his own recording label, which I thought was dope. I hated that my mom was on drugs, but I was grateful for my aunt Pat, who was my mom's sister. My aunt Pat was more of a mother to me than my actual mother, but no matter what, I loved my mom to death. I wasn't sure what made her start doing drugs because my mom used to have it going on. Until I turned sixteen, that's when shit got bad. She lost her job and our home, and we had to go live with my aunt Pat and my cousin Brian.

Tasha walked in the living room ready to go. I looked up, and Tasha was wearing a burgundy sweater, a pair of black jeans, and a pair of burgundy boots and she put her hair in a high ponytail. Tasha was looking so fucking good and when she smiled at me it made me feel things I never felt before.

"You look really beautiful, Tasha," I told her while licking my lips.

"Thanks, Cameron. Now, are you ready to eat because I'm starving," Tasha stated while grabbing her coat and bag. We got to Friday's in no time at the speed I was doing. I was enjoying listening to Tasha sing along to the songs on the radio. Tasha had a one of a kind voice, and I had no doubt that my brother had the skills to take Tasha to a place she couldn't even imagine going. Once we left

Friday's, we ended up spending the rest of the day together chilling and having crazy sex.

*****

The next morning, I woke to the smell of breakfast cooking. I looked over and didn't see Tasha in the bed. I went in the bathroom and handled my hygiene then went to find out what Tasha was in my kitchen whipping up. When I got down there, Tasha was singing and moving to her own tune. I didn't say anything at first. I just stood there and watched as she sang, danced and flipped pancakes.

"Are you having a good time in here?" I asked, sneaking up on Tasha, and she jumped.

"Cameron, you scared the shit out of me. I was just about to come get you to let you know that breakfast was ready."

"My bad, ma. I didn't mean to scare you. What you in here whipping up?"

"I made some pancakes, sausage and cheese eggs," Tasha replied.

"Damn, I'm about to fuck this food up. Well, if it's good," I said playfully.

"Nigga, I can cook, so trust me it'll be good," Tasha stated, sitting my plate in front of me. I couldn't front; that shit looked good as hell. Tasha sat down with her plate then blessed the food before we dug in. The first bite had me ready to propose to a bitch. I know that sounds extreme, but Tasha put a whole new taste on breakfast.

"Damn, ma, this food hitting. Where did you learn how to cook?"

"Honestly, I taught myself. My mom was a whore when I was growing up, so she was always in the streets, leaving me to fend for myself. I knew I had to eat, so I did what I had to do. If you think this meal is something, wait until I cook you some dinner."

I just nodded, listening to her story. Hearing her talk about her mom made me think about my mom. I could see now that shorty had the ability to make me fall for her, so I knew I was gonna have to fall back because I wasn't ready to be serious with anyone right now.

Chapter Four

Nyla

"So, Nyla, let's start off slow. What exactly is the nature of your nightmares?" Dr. Bridgette asked. I froze up because I wasn't ready to open up yet, but I knew I had to in order to move forward.

"Well, every time I close my eyes, bits and pieces of the night I was attacked comes back to haunt me as if it were happening all over again. Everything is so clear except for the man that did it."

"I know this is hard for you, but can you tell me some of the things that you see or hear in your dreams? Or if you just want to tell me what you remember from that night?" Dr. Brigette asked. I decided to just open up because that was the only way through this.

"I remember just graduating high school, and me and my best friend was excited about the school trip that was taking place at the Pocono's. At first, my brother wasn't too fond of me going, but he finally lightened up and gave his approval. When we got to the Pocono's, me and Tasha were having a ball. We were both drinking and partying like typical teenagers. Tasha ended up talking and chilling with this guy that went to another school, so eventually, she left with the guy, leaving me by myself. An older guy who didn't look much like a high school graduate came up to me and asked if he could get me a drink, but I declined. He didn't seem so happy with me, and he called me a stuck-up bitch. I remember cursing him out badly for calling me a bitch.

"You gonna regret that you stupid bitch," he threatened while walking off.

I picked up my glass of soda and finished it off. Moments later, I started to feel weird. I couldn't describe the feeling if I wanted to, I just got lightheaded, and I remember all I wanted to do was lay down. I tried to call Tasha, but she didn't answer. So, I made my way outside trying to get some air."

I paused, getting a little upset at the story.

"Just take your time Nyla, what happened next?" The therapist asked.

"That's the thing, everything went black from that point. I could hear voices, but I don't remember seeing anything. Just heard some voices," I told her.

"Okay, so can you tell me what you heard?"

"Just lay her stuck-up ass right there and fuck her crazy, Zeek. We're gonna stand here, watch you put in that work and then you'll officially be one of us."

"Man, I didn't sign up for no rape?" The guy said. I tried to talk, but I couldn't open my mouth.

"Nigga, who said anything about rape? I gave her something, so she won't remember a thing. Zeek, just do it. 'Cause if you don't, then we'll have to kill you because I can't afford for you to run your mouth."

"Man, get that gun off of me. This shit ain't even necessary; just give me a condom," the guy replied. Hearing him say something about a gun really had me shook.

"Are you saying that the guy that attacked you was forced?" Dr. Bridgett asked me.

"Yes, from what I can remember," I mumbled.

"Okay, go on." I took a deep breath before continuing. My chest started getting tight.

"The guy started to tug at my pants, and I begin to move around a little bit to get away from him."

"If that bitch keeps moving, slap the shit out of her," someone yelled.

"Please stop, don't do this to me. I'm a virgin," I pleaded lowly.

"I'm sorry he has a gun pointed at me and says he'll kill me. I don't want to die, but I swear I'll be as gentle as I possibly can. I promise. I don't want this no more than you do," the guy said into my ear.

"He didn't lie about being gentle with me. I laid there crying uncontrollably as I lost my virginity to a man that I had never seen in my life. I was scared and crying because I couldn't believe that something like that was happening to me.

"Okay, let's take a small break," the therapist requested.

"I would like to keep going," I told her.

"Are you sure?" I just nodded my head and continued my story.

"Man, you slow stroking her like she's your fucking woman. Nigga, fuck her like the whore she is," the angry guy yelled.

"As a matter of fact, get the fuck up and let me get some of that pussy."

"And that's when all hell broke loose. I started screaming and hollering. He pulled the guy that was on top of me off and climbed on top of me. I didn't want that man touching me. Even though I was being raped, I'd rather it had been the one that was doing it to me instead of the other guy. I knew he would make my life hell and he did.

As soon as he got on top of me, I heard him putting a condom on before he rammed himself inside of me. I screamed, and he hit me with the gun, and from there, everything went black. When I came to, I was in the hospital somewhere in the Poconos. Feeling lost and confused without a familiar face in the room," I cried.

"I know that you said you wanted to keep going, but I really think you need to take a break. This has never happened to me before, but I honestly need a break from this. I think we should pick back up tomorrow," Dr. Bridgette expressed her concern, and this time, I didn't object.

"I think you're right. I'll see you tomorrow at the same time," I told her while grabbing my belongings. When I got to my car, I sat there crying, thinking about that night. For some odd reason, thoughts of the first guy crossed my mind, and I wondered what happen to him or if that guy did something to him.

I finally got myself together and pulled off. When I got home, I didn't feel like being alone, so I decided to call Zaire. Zaire and I have been spending a lot of time together. Shit was starting to feel like it was getting serious. We were together damn near every day, not to mention at this point we've been on countless dates. We haven't had sex because I wasn't ready for that yet, but we did make out a few times. I dialed Zaire's number and he picked up on the first ring.

"Hello? Hello?" I said into the phone, but Zaire didn't say anything. I was about to hang up the phone until I heard voices in the back.

"Zaire, I knew you would miss this pussy. What your little girlfriend that you tried to play me for got some wack pussy? Or did she play you and haven't gave you none yet?" I heard the girl ask and my heart sunk.

"Sharee, don't come in here talking no shit before I change my mind, and who said anything about fucking you? I just want some head. I told you I ain't fucking your crazy ass no more, so get over here and suck this dick," Zaire said to the girl.

"Zaire, you got the game fucked up if you think I'm just gonna suck your dick and that's it. If I'm not getting fucked, then I ain't sucking no dick," the girl sassed.

"Just get your ass over here. You don't run shit over here," Zaire stated.

I couldn't take it anymore, and I hung up the phone because my heart was crushed. I mean, him and I hadn't made it official, but we were definitely dating, or so I thought. I felt so stupid. I needed my sister, so I called her. Ariel answered on the first ring.

"Hey, Nyla. Wassup? I was just about to call you to see if you wanted to shoot over to Brandon's with me for a little bit."

I didn't bother answering; I just cried. "Nyla, what the hell is wrong with you? Why are you crying?"

"Just come pick me up," I cried into the phone. Minutes after hanging up with Ariel, My phone rang, and I figured it was my brother. I was sure Ariel had called him by now, but surprisingly, it was Zaire. I sent his ass straight to voicemail. I had nothing to say to him now or ever again. Ariel called and said she was outside. I grabbed my things and headed out the door. When I got in the car, the ride to Brandon's was quiet.

"So, are you gonna tell me what happened or what?" Ariel asked.

"I'll tell you when we get to Brandon's. I don't feel like telling the story twice," I told her honestly. My phone rang again, and it was Zaire, but I swiped his ass again.

As soon as we walked in the house, Brandon didn't waste any time grilling me.

"What the fuck happened to you, Nyla? Why were you crying when you called Ariel?" My brother quizzed like he was my father.

"I called Zaire and heard him cheating on me. Some girl was about to suck his dick, and she wanted to fuck, and he was all for it. The girl even mentioned me. She asked was my pussy wack or was I not giving him none? He just told her don't start no shit and just suck his dick. How could he do this to me?" I cried.

"Nyla, when did the two of you make it official?" Brandon asked, catching me off guard. I got quiet for a moment and just looked at him for a moment.

"Well, we didn't actually talk about it, but I just assumed we were with all the time we spend together," I replied honestly.

"Nyla, you can't just assume y'all are together, and another thing, are you fucking him?"

"No, I'm not fucking him," I snapped, not understanding where my brother was going with these questions.

"Well, that's why he was about to get his dick sucked," Brandon stated, causing my heart to sink and my anger to rise.

"Brandon!" Ariel yelled.

"Nah, I'm sorry that your feelings are hurt, but you need to hear this. Ain't no man gonna sit around waiting on no pussy, especially since it's so much pussy out there that's willing to fuck. Niggas has needs too. Nyla, I understand that you were raped, but that was seven years ago. You have to learn how to move past that so you can live your life.

Therapy is just one part of the process, but it's more to it than just that. You got this man dating you and spending damn near everyday with you, and you're only thinking about yourself. I can tell that he's really feeling you. Have you even told Zaire why you haven't fucked him yet?"

"Brandon, I think you're being a little harsh," Ariel said.

"Nah, I'm just keeping it real. We just talked about this the other day, and you agreed we've been babying her a little too much. I'm sorry if my delivery isn't the greatest, but it's time to keep it real. Nyla, I'm not trying to make you feel bad, but you're dealing with something, not him. Especially since you didn't even tell him. I don't think he cheated. He's horny and you not giving up the goods, so you left him with no choice."

"So that's how y'all feel, huh? Well, you know what? Fuck both of y'all. I can't believe the shit you just said to me. Brandon, you're supposed to be riding for me, not against me. Apparently, y'all been doing some talking behind my back. Well, keep talking. I'm outta here!" I yelled while storming out the door. Ariel tried to holla after me, but I just ignored her and kept it pushing. The hell with both of them.

★★★★★

It's been two weeks since that shit went down with me and my siblings over Zaire. After thinking about everything that Brandon said to me, deep down, I knew he was right. I needed to move past my attack. I still haven't talked to Zaire, and I didn't have any desire to talk to him. I know I should at least hear him out, but I just wasn't ready yet. I heard my phone buzz that I had a text. I looked down at the phone and saw that it was a message from Zaire.

Zaire: Nyla, I'm not really sure what your problem is, but I haven't heard from you in two weeks, and I think it's rude to ghost a nigga without an explanation. I mean, if you don't wanna fuck with a nigga no more, just tell me. But don't just ghost me like I'm a nobody.

I read Zaire's text a few times debating if I should respond or not.

Me: You're right, that was rude of me. If you want to talk come over to my place around six, I should be home by then.

Zaire: Cool. I'll be there.

I didn't bother to reply back. I parked my car and headed into see my therapist. When I walked into her office, she is finishing up with a phone call. As soon as she hung up, she directed her attention to me.

"Well, hello, Miss Nyla. I thought you quit since I haven't heard from you since our first session."

"I'm sorry I just been going through some things and didn't feel like being bothered with anyone."

"Would you like to tell me what happened?" I thought about if I wanted to open up about what took place and decided why not. This is what I pay her for. Why not get my money worth.

"Well, first when I left here that day, I called a guy that I have been dating for two months and when his phone picked up, I heard him with another woman that he was about to have sex with. When I went to talk to my brother and sister about it, my brother kinda snapped on me and told me that I was being selfish since I wasn't having sex with the guy, and I wasn't honest with him about why I haven't. My brother and sister think that I let my attack stop me from having a future. That's just a summed-up version of the story," I told her. Dr. Bridgette wrote down a few things in her book before she spoke.

"I didn't know that you were dating. So, let's start with that. Tell me about your relationship with the guy you're dating."

"You mean the guy I was dating. Well, he was the first guy that has made it this far with me. I actually like him a lot and I believe he really likes me too. But hearing him with a woman broke my heart and I haven't spoken to him since."

"So, you just broke it off? Did you at least tell him why?" I just shook my head. I guess I was being ridiculous. Well, that's not fair, Nyla. Do you think there's any truth to what your brother and sister said?"

"I guess it's somewhat true," I told her.

For the next hour, we talked about a little bit of everything. I was happy I decided to come to therapy. It was really helping me see things in a different light. I would deal with my issues with Zaire tonight and Brandon and Ariel tomorrow. I missed my brother and sister like crazy. This was the first time we ever stopped talking and I knew I was being stubborn.

When I got home, Zaire was already parked in front of my door, waiting for me. For some reason, my nerves in my stomach were doing backflips, and I had to do a breathing technique that my therapist suggested I do when I felt like this. Surprisingly, it was working.

When my eyes connected with Zaire's, I almost forgot why I was even mad at him. I got out the car and walked into the house with him right behind me. Neither of us saying a word to one another. I closed the door, and Zaire wasted no time getting to the point.

"Nyla, what the fuck is going on?" he asked, skipping the small talk.

Well, hello to you too, Zaire."

"Nah, let's not get all formal now. Just tell me what's up?"

"Zaire, I heard you on the phone about to fuck some girl. I was on the phone when y'all started talking. Zaire looked shocked by my words. He took a deep breath before speaking.

"Nyla, if you were on the phone, then you would have known that ain't shit happened between us, and I sent her own her way. Yes, I'll admit that I was gonna let her suck my dick, but that's all that was gonna happen. But I didn't even let her do that. Nyla, I like you a lot, and I thought shit was getting serious with us, but you don't seem like you're interested in having sex with me. I'm a man and I have needs, Nyla." I felt like shit hearing him say that nothing happened between him and that woman. I felt like it was time to tell Zaire why we haven't had sex yet.

"Zaire, please have a seat. There is something that I need to tell you." Zaire did as I asked, sat on the couch, and I sat beside him.

"Zaire, the reason why I haven't had sex with you yet is because I'm scared. About seven years ago, I was drugged and raped by multiple men, and I was a virgin. I would never get that back. Those men took away my right to give my virginity to whoever I wanted to give it to." Zaire was wearing an unfamiliar face. He wrapped his arm around me and held me tightly as I cried in his arms.

"Baby, I am so sorry that this happened to you. Did they get arrested?" Zaire asked.

"There was no one to arrest. I couldn't remember their faces. I could only remember things that was said. But yeah, that's why we haven't had sex. Don't get me wrong; I wanted to have sex with you. I just wasn't ready, but I'm willing to try if you promise to be patient with me. My entire life I dreamed of the fairytale of being married first, then losing my virginity on my honeymoon, but obviously, that right was stolen from me."

"Baby, I am truly sorry. I just wished you had told me earlier. So, is this the real reason you want to open up a center for rape victims?" Zaire asked. I was shocked he even remembered that I told him that. I just nodded my head yes and buried my face into his chest. "Baby, no need to cry. I got you from here on out, I promise. And how I see it is even though you were assaulted, it wasn't with your permission, so it doesn't count. So, you still have the say so, and if you want to be married before you give it up, then make it happen." I never looked at it that way before, but he was right. If I didn't want to have sex until marriage, that was my right.

"Thank you so much and thank you for understanding, Zaire."

"It's all good. I guess I'll just have blue balls until you decide if a nigga is worthy enough for your hand in marriage," Zaire joked.

I thought about what Zaire said about him being worthy enough, and a small part of me was excited that he was feeling me enough to think about marrying me. That ten-minute conversation only made me like him ten times more than I already did. It was something about Zaire that gave me comfort and peace whenever I was with him.

Chapter Five

Zaire

Shit has been going pretty good with me and Nyla since she told me about her being raped. That was a little over a month ago. I had fell for Nyla pretty hard, and the more I was around her, the harder it was becoming for me not to have sex with her. Nyla was perfect in every way. I had no doubt in my mind that she was the one for me, but I didn't want to scare her off by asking her to marry me in just three months. Hell, I wasn't even sure that I was ready myself. I just knew that I wanted to be with Nyla. I knew it would be a long shot, but I planned on talking to Tasha today when she came into the studio so I could see what she thought my chances were with her best friend. The way I see it Tasha would probably know before me since that's her best friend.

I just pulled up to my mom's crib. I missed her like crazy and hoped every day that I would visit her and she would be drug-free, but for now, that was just wishful thinking. As soon as I pulled up, I walked around to the back to where Terrell usually be chilling at. Terrell was the dude I had looking after my mom.

"Hey, Zaire. Wassup?"

"Is everything good with my mom? Ain't nobody fucking with her, are they?" I asked.

"Nah, your mom's is straight. Actually, here some of your money back. She still gets high, but not as much as she used to. I didn't want to rob you, so I sat money to the side." I looked at that nigga with the side-eye because he had to be an honest nigga to give me money back, but this was his lucky day because I was gonna let him keep it anyway. I was happy as hell when he said my mom's habit slowed down.

"Aight, good looking. I'm about to go see her now, and go ahead and keep that money. I appreciate your honesty, man," I told Terrell before heading up to my momma's apartment.

I didn't bother to knock. I just used my key as I always did. When I walked in, I couldn't hide the surprised look on my face if I wanted to. The house was clean, and I could smell pine throughout the house. My mom had music on, and I couldn't believe what I was seeing, I followed the smell of food into the kitchen, which is where I found my mother.

"Hey, lady. How are you?" I asked, walking up on my favorite lady.

"Hey, baby. Your momma is good, how are you? And where the hell is my other son?" She replied.

"I believe he's at work. What's going on in here? You got it looking and smelling good in here," I told her.

"Yeah, I've been trying to get my shit together day by day. I've been smoking that shit for so long that I stop being a mother and a working woman. Now I'm not there yet, but I am at least trying," my mom stated. Hearing my mom say she was trying to get her shit together brought tears to a nigga eye.

"I'm so happy to hear that, mom. Just say the word, and I'll put you in a program. If you don't mind me asking, what happened that made you want to stop?"

"Honestly, Zaire, it was you." I looked at her with a surprised look on my face, wondering what the hell did I have to do with her stopping.

"I know you've been paying for my drugs, and before you go off, no he didn't tell me shit. But I'm not slow. Ever since that night y'all saw Rell rough me up, I haven't had to pay for my drugs. So, I figured you were paying for them or you threatened him to give me them for free. Either way, I knew it was you, and you had to be really scared for my life to pay for my drugs. So, thank you, and I will be taking you up on your rehab offer. Also, I want you to come back by the apartment later for dinner and make sure Cameron's with you. I need to talk to the both of you," my mother said.

She didn't have to tell me twice because I couldn't remember the last time I had my mother's cooking, let alone a real conversation. I didn't know how to feel or act. I mean, I was happy as shit, but I also wasn't used to this.

"Aight, momma. I'll be here with bells on," I joked, trying to lighten the mood. My mom just smiled then damn near put me out.

"Aight, son. Gone on ahead and get going. I'll see y'all tonight," my mom said with a smile. I did as she asked after kissing my mom on the cheek.

"I love you, mom."

"I love you too, Zaire. Now go on and get out of here, so I can make everything nice for you and your brother." I left out my mom's apartment and got to my studio in no time since I didn't work too far away from my mom's apartment. When I walked in the office, Sharee's ass was eye-fucking me.

"Zaire," Sharee stated sarcastically.

"Hello to you too, Sharee. Do I have any messages?" I asked.

"Nope, but you do have two women with smart ass mouths in your office waiting on you," she stated then rolled her eyes. I swear Sharee was standing on one leg at this job. I don't know why she didn't think I would fire her ass.

"Sharee, you're making it easier every day to fire your ass. You better act like you know who the fuck I am," I threatened before walking into my office.

When I walked into my office, I was shocked that Nyla was here with Tasha. This was the third time that Tasha had been here at the studio, but Nyla has never come.

"Hey, baby. I'm surprised to see you here today, but I'm glad that you came," I greeted Nyla, kissing her on the lips.

"Yeah, I decided to come out and support my bestie, and I wanted to check out my man's work scene. Your little fan out there almost got punched in her face," Nyla replied, returning the kiss.

"Well, Tasha, let's get started. I was up all night finishing this song and beat," I told Tasha. The three of us walked down to an empty booth and got started. I played the beat while she read the lyrics and let her take it away. Just like I thought, Tasha ripped that song. She did more with it then I thought it would be. I was for sure this was gonna be a hit.

"Yo, you really ripped that shit. You might as well get ready for your life to change with this hit song." Tasha was a natural. We've been working together for a few months, but she was mainly doing hooks and covers until I was able to write her a song.

"Bestie, you did your thing in there. I think we about to be rich," Nyla chimed in, causing both of us to laugh.

But Nyla was right, Tasha was about to be rich. That was the song that was gonna get her out the hood.

"Zaire, you wrote that song? I didn't know you could write like that," Nyla said.

"Honestly, writing is what I love to do. I work with a lot of artists and I write a lot of songs for some of y'all favorite artists. But anyway, Nyla, do you mind if I talked to Tasha alone for a second? You can wait in my office." As soon as Nyla walked out, I got straight to the point with Tash.

"Wassup?" Tasha asked before I had a chance to say anything.

"Look, I know I may be asking you to break the woman code asking you this, but I need to know. I love Nyla a lot, and I want to ask her to be my wife, but I don't know how she really feel about a nigga. I don't wanna get played, so do you think she'll say yes?" Tasha had excitement written over her face, and she couldn't hide it if she tried.

"Hell yeah, I think she'll say yeah. That girl loves you to death, but she thinks you don't want to fuck her because she was raped," Tasha stated, and that last part broke my heart. That was never my intention.

"Hell nah. The reason I haven't had sex with Nyla yet is because I wanted to make her fairytale come true. She told me that her dream was to lose her virginity on her honeymoon, so I think that she deserves to have that with the man of her choice. I'm gonna ask her to marry me on her birthday, but I need your help, so I'll be in touch," I told her.

"Ah, that's so sweet. Thanks for loving my friend through her pain, and I think that would be a great idea. Just make sure you ask Brandon for her hand in marriage."

"Yeah, I got that covered. Thank you so much. I just hope she doesn't play me out," I said seriously.

"I doubt that she will say no. Just relax," Tasha told me. "Also, that song really bangs, but let me get out of here before Nyla grows suspicious. Besides, you only have two weeks to handle your affairs and let me know if you need help picking out her ring," Tasha said with excitement laced in her voice.

"No doubt." I walked back into my office and Nyla was in her phone.

"Hey, babe, I may be over a little later tonight because I have to go over to my mom's place when I leave here. So, I'll call you when I'm on my way," I told Nyla, placing a kiss on her forehead before walking her and Tasha out.

*****

Later that evening, me and Cameron was pulling up to my mom's and I couldn't hide my excitement for being here. I didn't tell Cameron that my mom was cooking dinner for us and that she wanted to talk. I just told him I wanted him to go with me to check on her.

"Damn, somebody cooking something good. Nigga, I ain't gonna be here long 'cause a nigga hungry as hell," Cameron said. I didn't even bother to respond to his comment. I stuck my key in the door and the aroma for the food made my stomach growl. "What the fuck is going on in here?" Cameron asked loudly as he looked around the living room, noticing how clean it was.

"Hello, my favorite guys," my mom spoke.

When I looked up, I damn near choked on my saliva from the way my mom looked. I haven't seen my mom look that good in years; I forgot how beautiful my mother was. For years, my mom looked like a crackhead. Her hair was always on top of her head and her clothes were dingy. My mom was wearing a black tight fitted romper that showed the curves that I thought the crack would have taken away. She wore loose curls and light makeup. I was gonna make sure to get a picture in case this was the last night I saw her look like this.

"What the hell is going on in here, mom? You look beautiful," Cameron stated, surprisingly.

"Come to the kitchen. I just wanted to cook my sons some dinner and talk to y'all about a few things. I think it's about time for me to come clean about some things," my mother stated, making me raise an eyebrow. I was super curious about what my mom had to say. If it as anything bad, I hoped she waited until after we ate, so whatever she had to say didn't ruin my appetite because a nigga was starving.

Chapter Six

Cameron

When I walked into my mom's house, I couldn't believe my fucking eyes. The house was spotless, and the aroma from the food that she had cooked could be smelled from outside. But nothing topped her walking out looking the way she did. My mom was beautiful in every way. I couldn't hide how shocked I was even if I tried to. Me and Zaire fucked that food up that my mom made; she even made us a plate to go. She cooked fried chicken, steak, baked mac and cheese, collard greens, and her sweet cornbread that I always loved as a kid.

"Well, now that y'all finished eating, let me get to why I called you two here tonight. For starters, I just want to say thank you for not giving up on me while I let drugs take over my life, forcing Pat and Brad to take care of both of y'all. I love you two more than life itself, and I hated that I let drugs take over my life, causing me to lose the only thing that mattered to me. Especially to the two people I hate the most," my mom stated with so much hurt laced in her voice. I was really confused because why would she hate her own sister? If it weren't for my Aunt Pat and Uncle Brad, I don't know where we would be in life. Hell, we would have probably been in the system, and they probably would have separated me and Zaire.

"Mom, why would you say you hate Aunt Pat and Uncle Brad when they're the ones that took care of us when you got hooked on drugs?" Zaire asked, taking the thoughts right out of my head.

"Look y'all, I'm not gonna beat around the bush with y'all, and it's just time that the truth comes out. Brad is y'all father. Him and I fucked around for damn near three years before I found out about him and Pat, and by then it was too late. I had the biggest crush on Brad ever since we were younger. We finally started dealing with one another, but no one knew about us. Brad didn't want his business in the streets because he was five years older than me. Well, that's what he had me believing. Then after I had you, Zaire is when I found out that Pat was pregnant with her first kid. I was so happy that I was going to be an auntie until I found out that it was by Brad. Brad was the love of my life and I never got over him. Eventually it ate at me so bad that I started getting high to numb the pain," my mom stated.

"Why would she mess with the same dude her sister had kids by?" Zaire asked.

"She didn't know," my mom cried.

"Well, she obviously didn't care one way or another. She still stayed with him after she found out," I stated angrily.

"That's the thing Pat, has no idea that I've ever been with Brad," my mom cried.

"Mom, are you fucking serious? We've been living with our dad this entire time and no one thought we should know? Wait, are you saying that Brian is our brother and our cousin?!" I shouted angrily. My mom just nodded her head with tears in her eyes, and my blood started to boil. I jumped up, ready to head straight to my aunt's house, but my mom begged me to finish hearing her out.

"Cameron, I'm not finished. You've always been so hot-headed, and I see nothing has changed."

"Honestly, I don't want to hear anymore. I'm out," I yelled while storming out the door. My mom and Zaire were both yelling for me, but I wasn't beat to hear shit else. I drove straight to my Aunt Pat's house and banged on the door like I was the fucking police.

Bang! Bang! Bang!

"Who is it?" I heard Brian say through the door.

"Cameron?"

"Damn nigga, why the fuck are you banging the door down like that for?" Brian asked with a shit load of irritation in his voice.

"Where the fuck is Brad?" I yelled. Brian's eyes got wide and he looked scared.

"What the fuck is going on in here?" Brad asked, walking into the living room with my Aunt Pat right behind him.

"Yo, how could you do that slimy shit to my mom?" I aggressively asked while walking up on Brad, ready to punch his fucking lights out.

"Yo, what the fuck are you talking about, Cameron?" Brad asked with wide eyes. The entire room was silent.

My Aunt Pat and Brian was just looking at me trying to figure out what the fuck was going on, but the wait was about to be over because I wasn't holding shit back.

"Nigga, you know what the fuck I'm talking about. Tell your wife and your son who me and Zaire daddy is. Nigga, tell them," I yelled. "As a matter of a fact, I'll tell them. Sorry, Aunt Pat, but your no-good ass, low down husband is our dad. Yeah, he was fucking with my mom on the low because of her age. Then started fucking you too and broke my mom's heart when he stopped fucking with her after you found out you were pregnant with Brian!" I yelled, shoving Brad. I had spit flying out of my mouth. That's how pissed and hard I was yelling.

"What the fuck is he talking about, Brad?"

"Man, I don't know what the fuck this nigga talking about. Probably some lies his crackhead mother done told him," Brad said.

I lost it and punched that nigga dead in his face. Brad stumbled backwards then tried to rush me, but I dropped that nigga. Then I climbed on top of him and blacked out as I threw blow after blow. Brian was trying to pull me up, but there was no stopping me. The only reason I stopped when I did was because I heard Zaire and my mom's voice.

"Yo, what the fuck is going on in here?" I heard Zaire say. Zaire pulled me up off Brad.

"Nigga, have you lost your fucking mind coming up in my house with this bullshit? Then you put your fucking hands on me, nigga? I should kill your ass for that disrespectful shit," Brad threatened.

"Nigga, I would like to see you try. So, are you saying that you never fucked my mom?" I yelled.

"Cameron, calm down. This isn't the way to go about this. Brad, there's no reason to lie at this point. The kids are grown, and this was many years ago. I already told them everything," my mom calmly stated.

"Is somebody going to tell me what the fuck is going on in my damn house right now?" My Aunt Pat inquired confusedly.

"Look, I'm sorry to have to tell you this, but Cameron and Zaire are Brad's sons. Me and Brad was fucking around on the low for a minute. He claimed he didn't want anyone to know because I was too young. But I guess when he found out that you were pregnant, he decided he wanted to be with you, so he threatened to kill me if I said anything. He promised to still take care of the boys, and of course, I went with it because I was scared and in love. But over time, the heartbreak and pain were too much to bear, that's how I got hooked on drugs. I needed something to take away the pain and that's what the drugs did for me until they wore off. Then I was right back to being hurt. I'm sorry for all of this, and I should have been said something, but I didn't want to hurt you, Pat," my mom cried.

"Cameron, I know that you're hurt and upset, but I didn't tell you he was your father for you to come over here and do this. You've always been a hothead. But what's done is done, so let's get out of here and let them work their shit out. I had so much more to say, but we can continue our conversation some other time. It's just too much right now. Let's go boys now!" My mother stated. I was intrigued by her calmness because I would have been fucking shit up, but my mom was right. We needed to get out of there before I ended up in jail.

My aunt was trying to talk and get to the bottom of everything, but my mom wasn't beat tonight, so we left my Aunt Pat's. Zaire took my mom home because I needed to be alone. I wasn't in the mood to be around anybody.

As soon as I got in the house, I poured myself a double shot of 1800 and took a seat on the couch. I heard my phone ringing, and when I looked at my phone it was Tasha, I declined her call and turned my phone off. After drinking a few shots, I passed out right there on my couch.

Chapter Seven

Nyla

"How could he just ghost me like that, Nyla? Just last week shit was great with us, and now this week, he won't even return my calls. These niggas ain't worth shit these days," Tasha ranted about Cameron.

"Yeah, that shit is crazy. I can ask Zaire if he knows what's going on if you want me to."

"Nah, that's okay. I'll see his ass sooner than later. He can believe that."

Me and Tasha was at the mall getting me something to wear for my birthday, which was in three days. I wanted to look super cute and sexy. It's been a long time since I dressed up. My brother was throwing me a small get together, but I knew it was gonna be lit because anything that Brandon had his hand in was gonna be dope. Everything was great with me and my siblings since I sat them down and apologized for the way I behaved towards them for just being honest with me.

"Girl, that dress is bomb. That is the perfect dress for your birthday. My best friend about to shut shit all the way down," Tasha said while popping her ass in the middle of the store.

"Bitch, your ass is really retarded. Now all I have to find is some shoes and jewelry," I told Tasha while heading to the register to pay for my dress. After leaving out the store, we headed to the food court to grab something to eat before I continued shopping.

"So, how are things going with you and Zaire?" Tasha inquired.

"Actually, things are going great with us besides the fact that he won't have sex with me. I mean, he seemed like he was okay about me being raped, but he hasn't touched me yet."

"I mean, are you sure that you're ready to have sex with Zaire right now? I thought that you wanted to be married before you had sex. Have you changed your mind about that?" Tasha pried. I thought about what Tasha asked, and the truth was I did want to wait until marriage, but I doubted that Zaire would want to wait that long. Plus, being around him makes me super horny.

"Sometimes I feel like I'm sure I'm ready and other times I do want to wait until I'm married. But who the hell knows when the hell that would be? I really like Zaire. Actually, if I be honest with myself, I love Zaire. I never thought I'd see the day that I would hear myself say no shit like that, but it's true. He makes me happy," I told Tasha honestly.

"Wow, that's big for you. I'm glad that Zaire makes you happy. I wish you the best because you damn sure deserve it."

"Thanks. Now enough of all this love stuff. I need to find my shoes," I told her, getting up from the table.

*****

Later that night, I was sitting home on my couch, scrolling through my Facebook page when I heard my doorbell. I wasn't expecting anybody, so I didn't know who it could be.

"Who is it!?" I yelled.

"Delivery," the person on the other side of the door answered. When I opened the door, it was a delivery guy standing there holding some beautiful white and yellow flowers. I wasn't sure what kind of flowers they were, but they were big and beautiful. I signed for the flowers with a big smile. Once I closed the door, I sniffed the flowers and sat them down so I could read the card.

I think about you every day all day, You make me wanna be a better man. I never thought I'd see the day that I would meet such a beautiful woman that makes me so complete. I could be with you for eternity. I hope you like the flowers.

Ps, I know I've never said it before, and I'm not sure how you feel about me but just wanted to let you know that I love you more than you could ever imagine.

Sincerely yours, Zaire.

The card was simple and sweet and brought tears to my eyes. I wasn't sure why I let my guard down when it came to Zaire, but I was glad that I did. I picked up the phone and dialed Zaire's number so I could thank him for the flowers and tell him that I love him too.

"Hey, Chocolate drop. Did you get the flowers?" Zaire quizzed.

"Yes, I got them, and they're beautiful. Zaire, thank you, and I love you too," I told him honestly.

"A nigga glad to hear that, Chocolate drop," Zaire replied. "Listen, I have to go. I'm finishing up at the studio, but I'll be done in about an hour, and I'll hit you right back. I love you, Chocolate drop."

"Okay. Talk to you soon, and I love you too, Mr. Price," I stated with a wide grin before disconnecting the call.

When I hung up, I put my flowers in some water then called Ariel. I wanted to tell her about the flowers and that we finally told each other that we loved each other, but her ass didn't answer. So, I hung up and called Brandon, but he didn't answer either.

I really didn't want to call Tasha just yet because I knew that she wasn't on great terms with Cameron. I needed to tell someone, but to my surprise, her ass didn't answer either. So, I gave up and took a shower before climbing into bed with a book. I figured I'd catch up on some reading while waiting for one of the four of them to call me back.

*****

It was now the next day, and I was still high off Zaire telling me that he loved me and the beautiful flowers that he sent. I was happy as hell at work all day long, and now I was on my way in to see my therapist. She was starting to feel more like a friend than a therapist. The only difference was I didn't have to pay Tasha to listen to my problems.

"Good evening, Miss Thompson. Am I missing something because you are glowing tonight? Did you and Zaire finally have sex?" My therapist asked with a smile.

"Good evening and no, we didn't have sex, but he did tell me that he loves me. He wrote it on the card that came with the bouquet of flowers that he sent. Then when we talked on the phone, he said it again."

"So, what did you do?"

"I told him that I loved him too, and it felt good because I actually do love him."

"I'm really happy for you, Nyla. You're making great progress; this is great news," Dr. Bridgette stated.

"Yeah, I feel good about him," I told her.

"I'm glad that you're moving forward. Maybe one day he can come and do a session with you," Dr. Bridgette suggested.

"Maybe in the near future, but for now, I'm good," I told her. I wasn't ready for that yet. I had to take baby steps.

"Okay, it's no pressure. Well, if you don't have anything else that you want to talk about, this session is over."

"Okay. I'll see you next week," I told her before exiting my therapist's office. My ass was so happy that I skipped to my car like a big ass kid in the candy store. I got in my car and headed home. I planned to see if I could get Zaire to finally have sex with me.

Chapter Eight

Zaire

"Nigga, you sure you really ready to propose to Nyla tomorrow? You ain't even fuck her yet. What if the pussy is trash?" Cameron asked.

"Nigga, I doubt if the pussy is trash, but I'm not marrying her for her pussy. I'm in love. Nyla completes me, so yes, I'm ready. And speaking of ready, what the hell is going on with you and Tasha? Why the hell did you just ghost her ass like that?" I asked my brother.

"Shit was just getting too real, and you know I ain't with all that love shit. I just want a nut here and there and make money. I already fucked her more than I should have. I mean, she cool, but I'm good."

"Nigga, you could have at least talked to the girl about it. Especially since you know that I'm with her best friend, that shit was rude. And what are you going to do tomorrow at the party? Because you know her ass is going to be there."

"I'll cross that bridge when I get there, but for now, I got other shit on my plate to worry about." After talking to Cameron's ass a little longer, I left to stop past my mom's house.

Everything's been fucked up and awkward with my aunt and Brian ever since everyone found out that Brad was our dad. Everyone kept their distance from one another, but I heard my aunt Pat left his ass. I ain't going to lie; my mom should have never let that nigga marry her sister without making sure her sister knew what was going on. So, in my opinion, my mom was just as much to blame as that sick bastard was.

How the hell do you have kids with two sisters and raise your sons as your nephews, knowing damn well we were his flesh and blood? That nigga is sick. Something still didn't seem right with the story, but I guess the truth will come out eventually.

Tomorrow was the big night, and I was starting to get nervous. I already had her ring and my speech down pack, but I was so scared she was going to turn me down. Hearing Nyla tell me she loved me was like music to my ears. I just hoped I wasn't rushing things. I loved her and didn't want to be without her, so why wait?

When I got to my mom's house, I used my key and walked in the house. I heard music coming from her bedroom, so I walked towards my mom's door, and against my better judgment, I opened the door.

"Hey, mom. Oh my God, mom!" I yelled, covering my eyes like a small child. I couldn't believe I had just walked in on my mom getting her back blown out by some big, brawly looking nigga.

"Fuck! Zaire, close the door!" My mom yelled. I flew back out the house because I was too traumatized to be there when they came out the room. *Who the fuck was that nigga she was fucking? I thought while scratching my head. That image will forever be embedded in my head.*

"Fuck," I yelled loudly in my car. I made a mental note to never use my key again unless it was an emergency. I needed to tell someone, so I called Cameron's ass. Since my day was fucked up, I figured I'll fuck someone's else day up.

"Yo, wassup?" Cameron answered on the first ring.

"Yo, I just walked in on your mom getting her back blown out by some big ass brawly nigga. That shit was horrific," I told Cameron.

"Nigga, why the fuck would you call me and tell me some stupid shit like that? Who the fuck was the dude?"

"I called you to fuck up your day like they fucked up mine, and I don't know who the hell he was. I left out the house, and now I'm just sitting in the car traumatized."

"Well, I don't want to hear that shit. Don't ever call me with no shit like that again," Cameron warned before hanging up in my ear. I got out the car to go back in the house, but I was just gonna wait in the living room until my mom came out.

I walked back in the house and grabbed something to drink out the fridge. Ever since my mom started her drug program, shit was starting to feel like they were before she got hooked on drugs. She kept the house clean and stacked with food. Finally, I heard the door open, and my mom and the big nigga came walking out the room smiling and shit. The guy reminded me of the dude from the movie, *Baby Boy*.

"Zaire, I'm sorry you had to see that, but you should have knocked first," my mom stated. I just rolled my eyes at her comment.

"Mom, who the hell is this nigga?" I asked, getting straight to the point.

"Zaire, I'm the parent, and last I checked, this was my house so don't come up in my shit questioning me like I'm a damn child. Now I hate that the two of you had to meet this way but Zaire, this is my boyfriend, Charles. Charles, this is my youngest son, Zaire," my mom introduced the two of us.

The Charles guy stuck his hand out for me to shake, but I was on my petty shit and left that nigga hanging.

"Zaire Price, you are being extremely rude right now, and you need to stop with this foolishness. I would expect this type of behavior from your brother but not you," she disapprovingly stated.

"My bad, mom, I was just caught off guard. I'm Zaire," I introduced, shaking his hand.

"It's nice to meet you, young blood. I've heard a lot about you and your brother. It's a pleasure to finally meet you."

"That's funny you heard about us because we don't know shit about you," I heard Cameron's voice say. The three of us turned to Cameron's direction.

"Don't come in here with that shit, Cameron. As a matter of fact, both of y'all give me my damn keys and sit y'all asses down!" My mom yelled. I guess she was tired of our shit.

"Look, like it or not, this is my boyfriend Charles, and he's gonna be around for a while, so y'all need to get y'all shit together. I'll have a dinner soon so the three of you can get acquainted. Charles, I'll see you tonight. Let me talk to my fathers for a minute," my mom sarcastically stated.

Before Charles walked out the door, him and my mom shared a kiss that turned my stomach. Cameron let out a loud sigh but knew not to say shit. Charles deepened the kiss then looked at us and smiled.

"It was nice meeting the two of you. I look forward to getting to know you," he stated smugly before walking out. That nigga had a lot of balls, but for some odd reason, I kinda liked how he handled the situation, but I'll keep that to myself.

"When the hell did the two of you become so disrespectful? You weren't raised that way," my mom asked.

"Mom, how would you know how we were raised? You were on drugs, remember? Or is everyone gonna pretend that shit didn't happen just because you're trying to get your shit together now? We still went through a lot, and you weren't the one who raised us, so a lot of shit has changed," Cameron expressed. I could see the hurt in my mom's eyes. I just wished that Cameron didn't push so hard because the last thing we needed was for her to start using again.

"Cameron, you need to chill the hell out. You're doing too much right now," I told Cameron. Ever since that night, he's been off the hook. I could barely recognize who he was anymore.

"I think the both of you should leave now. Just go now!" my mom yelled. Then she walked over to the door and held it open. I didn't feel like arguing with her, so we both got up and left. I prayed that she didn't go cop no drugs. I didn't either bother to say shit to Cameron. I just jumped in my car and peeled off with no destination in mind.

I decided to head to the mall to pick up a few things and clear my head. I wanted to call Nyla, but I decided against it. I would just wait until her lunch break. When I got to the store, I headed straight to the jewelry store for a new watch, earring, and a chain. I wanted to look good for the big day tomorrow. Once I was done all my shopping, I got in the car, pulled out my phone and dialed Nyla's number.

"Hey, baby," Nyla sang cheerfully into the phone.

"Hey, Chocolate Drop. How's your day going so far?"

"It's okay; it's just been busy all day. How's your day?"

"It started off rough, but I'm getting through it. Do you have any plans tonight?" I inquired.

"None that I know of. Is everything okay?" Nyla asked with concern laced in her voice.

"Yeah, I'm good. Just family shit, but I could tell you about it over dinner tonight."

"Sounds good. I'll see you tonight," Nyla said. After hanging up with Nyla, I decided to take my ass home and take a nap before going out with Nyla.

Chapter Nine

Tasha

I was trying to get dressed for Nyla's birthday, and surprise engagement party, but all I've been doing was crying all day long. After being sick all week long, I decided to go grab a pregnancy test. Well, four of them to be technical, when I realized that my period was late. After taking all four pregnancy tests, which all read pregnant, I've been super emotional. I didn't want to tell Nyla yet because I wasn't trying to ruin her day. And as bad as I wanted to call Cameron, I decided against it since he ghosted me. I haven't heard from him in damn near two weeks. I mean, no calls, texts or nothing. Now I'm pregnant by a nigga that won't even return my phone calls. There was no way in hell I could have this baby. I wasn't ready to be no mom. I was just getting my singing career off the ground. I wasn't sure how I was going to react when I saw Cameron tonight, but I knew that I was going to see him because this was an important night for his one and only brother.

I was now dressed and ready to head out the door, but of course, my unborn wouldn't allow that to happen. I ran to the toilet, praying I would make it on time without getting vomit on my clothes or shoes. If it wasn't for the fact that Nyla was my best friend, I would've taken this dress off and got in the bed with the way that I was feeling. I went into the kitchen and grabbed a ginger ale from the refrigerator, and some crackers that I was sure was stale.

I was not getting stuck in the house tonight. I was looking too good not to be seen. I was rocking a short, silver, lace dress and a pair of red and silver Louboutin's. My ass and thighs in this dress made me want to fuck myself. I decided to wear my hair layered, and my red curls brought out my yellow complexion. My stomach was finally settled, so I got in the car to head over to the party. As soon as I drove off, my phone started ringing, and Nyla's name came across the display screen in the car.

"Hello."

"Bitch, where the hell you at?" Nyla questioned.

"My bad, bestie. I'm on my way now. I got stuck in the bathroom, but I'm good now," I told Nyla.

"Just hurry up and get here," Nyla demanded.

"I'll be there shortly," I told her before disconnecting the call.

When I pulled up to the spot, I instantly got nervous because I knew I was going to see Cameron, and I wasn't sure that I was prepared to look him right now. I sat in my car for about three minutes, telling myself that everything was going to be just fine. I also said fuck that nigga a few times. I finally walked in and everything was absolutely beautiful. Everything was decorated in royal blue, white and gold. I located Nyla and my best friend was just breathtaking. I walked over to the table that she, along with Ariel and Brandon were sitting at. I scanned the room for Zaire and Cameron but didn't see them.

"Damn bestie, you look stunning. I can't believe how beautiful you look," I told Nyla, placing a kiss on her cheek. I spoke to Ariel before gazing into the eyes of my first love. I have loved Brandon since we were younger. Brandon actually took my virginity, but no one besides the two of us knew that. As bad as I wanted to tell Nyla, I just couldn't because she would have killed my ass. Nyla made it very clear that her brother was off-limits, so that would be one secret that I take to my grave.

"What's up, Tasha?" Brandon spoke coolly.

"Hey, Brandon. Wassup?" I spoke back.

"Tasha, you look gorgeous your damn self," Nyla complimented, causing me to blush.

"Thanks, bestie. Where's your man at?"

"You're welcome, and Zaire just texted and said he was on his way." I sat down at the table, trying to calm my sickness. I wasn't sure why I was nauseous at this hour. I thought it was called morning sickness not night sickness?

Twenty minutes later, I scanned the room once more, and this time my eyes landed on Cameron, who was looking so fucking good that I forgot that I was pissed at him. But I swear if I weren't pissed, I would have taken his ass home and gave him the business. I wasn't sure if I was staring too hard or what, but Cameron turned and looked directly in my direction. I tried to turn my head to act like I wasn't staring, but that didn't work because he was walking towards me. My heart was damn near beating out of my chest, not to mention I was praying that I didn't vomit from the nerves that were doing backflips in my pregnant belly. I closed my eyes and took a few slow breaths. When I opened my eyes, Cameron was standing in front of me looking so damn good that I could have sucked his dick right then and there.

"Hello, Tasha. You are looking good," Cameron complimented.

"Thanks. You're looking pretty dapper yourself." It took everything in me not to ask him why the hell he ghosted me the way he did, but I held my tongue.

"Look, I know how I went about shit was fucked up. I'm sorry about that. I was really going through some shit. If you're not busy after the party and if you're not too pissed at me, maybe we could talk?" Cameron asked, licking his lips. As much as I wanted to decline his offer for conversation, I just couldn't do it.

"Yeah, that's cool," I answered coolly, trying not to sound too desperate.

"Aight, cool," Cameron replied then kissed my cheek. 'I'll be over there at that table if you need me," Cameron stated before walking off.

It was in that moment that I realized that I had fallen for Cameron. I wasn't too happy about it since it was obvious that he didn't hold the same feelings that I did. But why would he have the same feelings? We've only known each other for a few months, and I was still trying to figure out where my feelings for him came about in such a short time.

Chapter Ten

Zaire

My nerves were doing backflips because it was now time to propose to Nyla. Nyla was beautiful to me for the first moment that I laid eyes on her, but it was something about her beauty that stuck out to me tonight. Nyla was wearing a long, gold sequenced, one-shoulder dress that hung on the floor in the back, but it had a high split in the front; all of her legs were out. The dress only covered her special jewel, yet the dress was sexy as hell. She was rocking a pair of open-toe gold shoes that matched her dress perfectly. It was something about the way the dress laid across on her perfectly chocolate skin. I couldn't wait to make Nyla my wife so I could finally feel her insides. If Nyla accepts my proposal tonight, I had no desire to wait to marry her. I planned to marry Nyla within the next two weeks. I walked over to the Mc to gain everyone's attention.

"May I have everyone's attention? First, I just want to say Happy Birthday, Nyla. It has been an honor celebrating your birthday with you tonight. I have a few surprises lined up that I would love to share with you. Brandon, could you please put the chair in the middle of the floor for me, please?"

Nyla was looking around, trying to figure out what the hell was going on. Brandon put the chair in the middle of the floor and Nyla took her seat.

Once she was seated, the DJ played the instrumental to "All Of Me" and on que, John Legend slowly walked out. When the crowd realized that John Legend was there singing, they began to scream and make ooh's and ahh's sounds. John Legend was now standing in front of Nyla, and she covered her face as he sang. When he finished his song, next up was the group, Next. They jumped right into their hit song, "Wifey." They had the crowd going wild. I made my way to the front where Nyla was sitting. She was looking around the room, trying to locate me and didn't realize that I was standing right next to her. As the song was coming to an end, I dropped down on one knee in front of her. My heart was beating so loud that I was almost sure that it could be heard over all the noise that was happening.

"Oh my God! Zaire, what are you doing?" Nyla asked with her hands still covering her face.

"Nyla, when I first laid eyes on you a few months ago at the movie theater, I knew I wanted to get to know you. Once I started talking to you, I knew that I didn't want to be without you. So here I am on one knee hoping that you'll grant my wish and be with me forever. Nyla, also known as my Chocolate Drop, will you make me the happiest man alive and be my wife? Before you answer, please know that I won't promise to be a perfect husband or promise that I won't ever make you cry or hurt you. Because they're impossible things to promise and I would be starting our future off with a lie if I tell you that. But what I can tell you is I will try my very best not to make you cry or hurt you. Nyla "Chocolate Drop" Thompson, will you be my wife?" I asked.

Nyla's long pause was starting to scare me. I prayed she wasn't about to turn me down because if she did, my soul would be crushed.

"Baby, say something; my knees are killing me, "I half-joked, causing the crowd to laugh.

"Zaire, I don't know what to say," Nyla cried. Someone from the crowd yelled, say yes.

"Yes, Zaire, I'll marry you!" Nyla answered. I was so happy that I didn't care who was watching us. I kissed my soon-to-be wife so passionately. "I love you so much, Zaire," Nyla said in between kisses.

"I love you more, Chocolate Drop." All I wanted to do was take her home and make sweet love to her beautiful ass, but I decided to just wait until we were married. Nyla deserved her fairytale, so that's what Nyla was going to get.

Chapter Eleven

Cameron

Shit with me has been crazy ever since that night that I found out that my supposed to be uncle was really my father. My mom didn't want to talk about it, but I think its way more to the story then she's telling us. I haven't been fucking with nobody like that. All I do is work and go home. I rarely even see Zaire like that. I just need a little time for myself to gather my thoughts. Brian and my Aunt Pat has been blowing up my phone, but I haven't been answering. I knew I wasn't being fair to them because they didn't do anything wrong and was more than likely calling to check up on me. I felt kinda bad with the way I just ghosted Tasha. She at least deserved a text back, but I was being stubborn and stuck in my ways. I knew I would see Tasha at the party, and I had no idea what I was going to say when I saw her.

When I first got to Nyla's birthday, I didn't see Tasha right away, but when I laid eyes on her, my damn eyes damn near popped out of my head. Tasha looked stunning and that shit had a nigga feeling weird in the inside. So, I knew I had to go over and break the ice. I was glad that she agreed to come chill with me after the party. I couldn't front, even though I was being stubborn, I missed Tasha like crazy. I was happy for my brother on his engagement, and I was glad that he found love. I thought it was too soon for marriage, but who was I to get in the way of their happiness? Besides, Nyla seemed like a good fit for my brother. After the party was over, Tasha kept her promise and came to chill with me. As soon as we got in the house, I gave her one of my shirts to put on so she could be more comfortable, and I changed as well.

"Cameron, why did you ghost me like that? I thought that we were cool.," Tasha asked, catching me off guard.

"Honestly, Tasha, I was going through something with my family, and I just didn't want to be bothered with anybody. I know that's no reason for the way I treated you, and I truly apologize for that." The room fell silent for a few moments before Tasha responded.

"You're right. That isn't an excuse for how you treated me, but I'll accept your apology under one condition," Tasha stated. I looked at her with raised eyebrows.

"And what condition is that?" I asked.

"That you promise to never do it again and that you tell me about it," Tasha said while rubbing my hand. I had to think about what she was asking because I wasn't the type to sit up and pillow talk with no chick. I was the hit it a few times kinda nigga and bounce, so this would be something new for me. But it was something about Tasha that made me wanna open up.

"That's fair. Well, for starters, my mom has been on drugs for years. Me and Zaire was raised by my aunt and my uncle, who my mom just told us that is our father. So, I lost it because that was some crazy shit to wrap my head around, so I kinda shut everyone out. I feel like my mom isn't being completely honest with me and my brother and its more to what she's saying. But what type of nigga fucks with two sisters, gets one pregnant, then turn around and marry the other sister?" I told Tasha, not holding anything back.

"Wow, I'm so sorry to hear that. Yeah, that is crazy," Tasha replied. I could tell that she didn't really know what to say, and I couldn't blame her because I was still trying to process everything myself.

"I know I don't know the full story, but what I do know is blocking the situation out like it doesn't exist isn't going to fix the issue. My suggestion would be that you call a family meeting and try to get to the bottom of all of this. Maybe you need to express how you're feeling instead of ignoring everyone." I thought about what Tasha said, and she was right. I guess I did need to get some shit off my chest.

"I feel you, Tasha, but I just don't think that I'm ready for all of that yet. Listen, I know I told you I wanted to talk, but I missed being inside of you, so if you don't mind, I would like to put this dick up in you," I told Tasha, straight up.

Tasha didn't reply with her words. Instead, she climbed on top of me and started kissing me. I didn't object because I was ready to feel her wetness. After kissing for what seemed like forever, I was finally deep inside of

Tasha's tight wetness. After fucking and making love for about two hours, we were finally done. I didn't have anything else left in me.

"Damn, that shit was good," I told Tasha, trying to catch my breath.

"Yeah it was. Cameron, I know this might not be the best time, but I need to tell you something," Tasha stated, gaining my full attention. Tasha took a deep breath and I was starting to get worried.

"Tasha, please don't tell me that you got something because I never had a disease in my life," I blurted, thinking the worst.

"Cameron, I don't have anything, but I am pregnant. I found out a few days ago when we weren't talking. I'm scared to death, and I don't know how to feel about this pregnancy," Tasha cried.

I was in utter shock and didn't know how to respond. I needed to gather my thoughts before I replied because I didn't want to come off as an asshole, but the last thing that I needed in my life right now was a baby.

"Tasha, I really don't know what to say right now without sounding like an asshole. I mean, don't get me wrong I like you a lot, but I'm not ready to be a dad," I told Tasha honestly.

"Well damn, Cameron, why don't you tell me how you really feel," Tasha said, jumping up from the bed.

"Tasha, I'm not trying to hurt your feelings. I just wanted to be honest with you. I mean, it's your body, and I can't force you to do something that you don't want to do, but if you were to get an abortion, I would pay for it. I'll even go with you if you want me to," I told Tasha.

"I don't need shit from you, Cameron. I'll let myself out. This the last time you'll hear from me," Tasha yelled while storming out. As bad as I wanted to go after her, I let her be. When I heard the door shut, I just laid in bed and put the pillow over my face until I drifted off to sleep.

★★★★★

When I woke up the next morning, I felt bad for how shit went with Tasha last night. I just laid there in bed with my hands behind my head, looking up at the ceiling.

How the fuck did I allow myself to get caught up and get Tasha pregnant? Ever since I started fucking when I was a young boy, I always made sure that I wore a condom. Tasha had me doing shit I wouldn't normally do with a chick. I contemplated on if I should call her or not, but I decided to give her some alone time. I finally got out of bed and took a shower so I could get to work. Today was Saturday, so I would only be there for a few hours. As soon as I got to work, I walked in my office, sat my things down, and turned on my computer so I could get my work down then get the hell out of there. After working for two hours, all I could think about was Tasha. That shit was eating at me, so I decided to text her.

Me: Tasha, I know you're probably pissed at me for what I said last night, but I was just caught off guard and would really like to talk about this.

Tasha: Cameron, please just leave me alone. You said exactly what you meant to say last night. But it's my fault I should have never said anything and just got rid of the baby. The only reason I said anything was because I got caught up last night, but you don't have to worry about me again. No need to respond, lose my number.

I read Tasha's text twice before tossing my phone on my desk. I really needed to get my shit together and quickly. I decided today was the day I was gonna get to the bottom of this mess with my family. I sent everyone a separate text telling them I needed to talk to them, but what they didn't know was all of them were gonna be in one room.

When I left work, I stopped to get something to eat because a nigga was hungry as hell. I wasn't sure what tonight's family meeting was going to bring, but I hoped that it at least gave us some closure and a better understanding about what the fuck was going on.

Chapter Twelve

Nyla

I couldn't believe that I was about to get married in two weeks. Zaire and I decided not to wait and get married right away. We planned a mini vacation to Costa Rica, and I couldn't wait. I wasn't sure if I was more excited about becoming a wife or was I happier because I was finally gonna get some dick. I didn't have anyone from my side that was coming, except my sister Ariel, my brother Brandon, and his girlfriend Mariah and of course, Tasha. With everything that was going on with Zaire's family, I wasn't sure who exactly was coming along, and I honestly didn't care. I wasn't trying to be rude, but the most important person was coming, and Zaire was all I needed. I had just pulled up to Tasha's house because I haven't really heard from her since my birthday. She would send me a few short texts here and there, but that was about it, so I decided to do a pop up on her ass. I knew Tasha well enough to know that something was wrong. I just wasn't sure what it was.

When I pulled up to her house, I was glad to see that her car was parked outside. I knocked on the door, and after knocking for a few minutes, Tasha finally answered the door. She looked like she just woke up, which made me look at my watch because I was sure it was almost one in the afternoon, and she looked like this was the first time she's been up today.

"Nyla, what are you doing here? Is everything okay?" Tasha asked, wiping the crust out of her eye.

"I came to see my best friend, are you just waking up?"

"Yes, I'm just getting up. Why, is sleeping late a crime now?" Tasha asked sarcastically.

"Damn girl, what the hell is wrong with you? I was just asking a question. Move out the way, I'm coming in," I told Tasha, walking right past her. Once I was in, I sat down on the couch and waited for Tasha to join me. She went to the bathroom first then finally came to sit down. "Best friend, what the hell is going on with you? You seem so distant lately."

Tasha just looked at me and her eyes were teary. "I'm pregnant, Nyla, and when I told Cameron, he said he didn't want any kids and offered to pay for an abortion," Tasha cried.

"Oh my God, Tasha. Why the hell didn't you tell me? You don't have to do this alone. You have me, Tasha. Fuck Cameron. He can be such an asshole sometimes," I consoled Tasha, holding her tight.

"I found out on your birthday, and I didn't want to ruin your day, so I kept it to myself. I went home with Cameron after your party because he wanted to talk and apologize about the way he ghosted me. One thing led to another and we ended up having sex. It was different, and it felt like it meant something. I got caught up in the moment and told him, and he wasn't too happy about it. Cameron didn't consider my feelings for five minutes before the word abortion flew out of his mouth."

"Wow. I'm sorry, Tasha, but I can't let you go out like this. You look a mess. Go get dressed; I'm taking my best friend out to lunch," I told Tasha. She didn't object; she got up to go get dressed. While Tasha was getting dressed, I wondered if Zaire knew about the pregnancy. We pulled up to Friday's, and I couldn't wait to eat because I was hungry as hell. Once we were seated and finished placing our orders, I decided to pick my best friend's brain to see where she was at with this pregnancy.

"Tasha, I know this must be hard for you, but what do you want to do about this pregnancy? Do you want to keep the baby, or do you want to have an abortion?"

"I honestly don't know. I have mixed feelings, but I think I'm leaning more towards getting an abortion. I just don't think I'm ready to be a mom, and I for damn sure don't want to be a single mother. It's gonna be hard, but I'm just gonna make an appointment so I could get it over with and move forward," Tasha answered sadly.

"Just know that I'm here for whatever you decide. Just let me know when you're going to the clinic and I'll go with you," I assured my best friend. I hated to see her have to go through this. I was a little disappointed in Cameron but not too disappointed because this was the type of shit niggas did all the time.

"Thanks, Nyla. I really appreciate you. On another note, I can't wait to get to Costa Rica so we can turn up. I can't believe you're really getting married."

"Girl, yes, and I know this shit is crazy. I still can't believe I'm getting married. I can't wait to get some dick. I've never been so horny in my damn life," I told Tasha honestly.

"Girl, I bet, but the hell are you going to do if when y'all finally get it in its trash?" Tasha asked jokily, but that was something that I' hadn't thought about.

"Girl, I don't think that's possible, but I'll cross that bridge when I get there." After we were finished eating, I dropped Tasha back off at home and took my ass to therapy. Things had been going well with therapy to the point that I was considering inviting her to Costa Rica. I know that may sound a little crazy, but if it weren't for Dr. Bridgette, there is no way that I would have even considered dating, let alone would I have said yes to Zaire's proposal.

When I walked into Dr. Bridgette's office, she was just finishing up with a phone call. I sat down on the couch in my favorite spot.

"Good evening, Miss Nyla. How are you doing this evening?" Dr. Bridgette greeted.

"Good evening, Dr. Bridgette. I'm doing fairly good, just getting a little nervous about marrying Zaire. I don't know the first thing about being a wife. I'm still trying to learn how to be a girlfriend," I explained.

"Nyla, you'll do fine, so don't worry. And believe it or not, it is perfectly normal to be nervous. I've been married for fifteen years, and I was so nervous the day I married my husband that I almost didn't marry him. I created every excuse on why we weren't ready. But you got this, Nyla and Zaire seems great. Is there anything else on your mind that you'll like to discuss?"

"Not really. I know this may sound silly, but I was wondering how you would feel about coming to my ceremony in Costa Rica if you had the time to take off?"

"Oh, Nyla, that is so sweet. I don't think that would be very professional of me to attend, but I wish you the best on your special day. I'm sure you will look beautiful," Dr. Bridgette stated.

"Well, I guess I'll see you when I get back then," I told her while getting up from my seat.

"I have a better idea. Why don't you bring Mr. Zaire by the office on Tuesday, at 6 p.m. so I can meet this lucky guy? But I won't be at this office. I'll be at my Deptford office," Dr. Bridgette replied.

"That sounds good. Thank you so much, Dr. Bridgette. I don't know how I would have made it this far without you." She just smiled and wrote the address down. After taking the address, I headed out the door.

When I pulled up to my house, Zaire was pulling up at the same time that I was. A smile crept across my face. Whenever I saw Zaire, he gave me butterflies. I couldn't believe that I had found love and happiness.

"Hey, Chocolate Drop. Did you miss daddy?" Zaire flirted. Zaire picked me up and swung me around like you see people do on tv. He placed a kiss on my lips, and I gladly slid my tongue into his mouth. His tongue tasted like spearmint gum.

"Aight, let me put your thick ass down before I fuck your ass right here on this car," Zaire stated. He put me down and smacked my ass before walking into the house.

I couldn't wait to marry the man of my dreams in just a few short days.

Chapter Thirteen

Cameron

I was sitting at work thinking about the family meeting that we had. I knew it was more to my momma's story than that bullshit she tried to tell us. I couldn't believe that nigga raped my mom, and that's how I was conceived but how my momma fell in love with her rapist really had me fucked up. Finding out I was a rape baby really fucked me up and pissed me off. I haven't been fucking with anyone after the meeting, including Zaire. He didn't do shit to me, but I just didn't want to be bothered. I was sitting at my desk when my office door opened up and in walked Zaire.

"Yo, why do I have to pop up at your job in order to talk to my brother? I don't know why you shut me out. I haven't done shit to you," Zaire argued.

"Look Zaire, we just handle shit differently. You act like the shit don't bother you. I can't pretend like you," I snapped.

"Nigga, ain't nobody pretending, but I'm not about to let some shit that happened damn near thirty years ago get me all bent out of shape like I can fix the shit. Yes, I'm pissed and hurt, but what the fuck? Life goes on. All we can do now is figure out how to get past the hurt."

"Whatever you say, Zaire. Is that what you came here for?"

"You know what, Cameron? Fuck you! I'm sick of your shit. But why your ass in here acting like a little bitch, I just thought you should know that Tasha is on her way to the abortion clinic to kill your seed because of your selfish ass ways!" Zaire yelled before storming out of my office. I instantly felt like shit and didn't know what to do. I knew I was going through my own shit, but I hated hearing that Tasha was getting an abortion.

I pulled out my phone and dialed Tasha's number, but she didn't answer. "Fuck!" I yelled to myself. I jumped up from my desk, grabbed my things, and darted out the door. I didn't even know what clinic she was going to, but I had to find out and quick. I wasn't sure where things stood between Tasha and I, but I was sure that I didn't want her to get rid of my seed. Once I got in the car, I googled abortion clinics, and the closest one to Tasha was in Cherry Hill. So, I made that my first stop. When I pulled up, it was people standing outside, holding signs and shit. From what I could read, these people was against abortions. I walked into the clinic, looked around, and I couldn't believe how packed it was in there. I prayed that they performed other services besides abortions because this was insane. I didn't see Tasha, but when I scanned the room a second time, I spotted Tasha and Nyla sitting in the corner. I walked over stood in front of Tasha. When she looked up, she looked like she saw a ghost.

"Cameron, what the hell are you doing here? Nyla, did you call him?" Tasha asked in one breath.

"No, she didn't call me. I'm here because I don't want you to get rid of my baby. I know I acted like a fool and was being selfish, but please let's just talk about this," I pleaded.

"Cameron, there is nothing to talk about. I'm not ready to be a mother right now anyway. My mind is made up, so can you please leave," Tasha snapped.

I could see the tears forming in her eyes, and I knew that wasn't what she really wanted to do. I never had to beg a woman for anything a day in my life, so this shit was new to me. But something deep down told me that Tasha was the one, and if I didn't want to lose her, then I better sat my pride to the side.

"Look, Tasha, I know I act like I don't care about what we have, but I do. You're different from the other women that I've dealt with. This is me sitting my pride to the side and doing something that I've never done before. I'm begging for you to give me another chance to see that I'm not the asshole you think I am. Tasha, I don't know what the future holds, but what I do know is I can't imagine my future without you being in it. Please don't get rid of my seed," I pleaded.

I didn't know where the fuck all of this was coming from. I was sounding like my soft ass brother in this clinic with all these nosey ass bitches looking at me like I was crazy. Tasha just stood there staring with tears in her eyes.

"Tasha Smith," the nurse called. When Tasha got up to walk to the back, I grabbed Tasha's arm.

"Tasha, please don't do this!" I pleaded once more. My plea fell onto deaf ears because Tasha went to the back with the lady.

"I'm so sorry, Cameron," Nyla stated while shaking her head.

"It's not your fault, but I tried. I can't stay here for this, tell Tasha to call me if she needs anything," I said to Nyla before walking away.

"Cameron, wait!" I heard Tasha's voice call out as I was walking to my car. When I turned around, Tasha was jogging towards me with Nyla right behind her. I met her halfway and hugged her tightly.

"I couldn't do it, Cameron. I just couldn't do it," Tasha cried into my arms. I kissed the top of her forehead, relieved that she didn't get rid of my seed. Nyla stood there beside us. I guess making sure her best friend was good.

"You can leave her with me, sis. I got it from here," I assured Nyla.

"Aight, I'm out. Tasha, call me whenever you get some free time."

"Thanks for not getting rid of my kid, Tasha."

"Cameron, did you mean everything that you said about us?" Tasha inquired.

"I meant every word of that I said. Now, let's go get something to eat. A nigga is starving after all that begging I had to do to for you be my girl," I stated, hoping that she caught on to what I was trying to ask her.

"Wait, so that's what I am? I'm your girl now?"

"Well yeah, if that's okay with you. I really want to know where this could go. Besides, we are about to have a kid together." Tasha just smiled at my comment. All I could think about was how grateful I was that Zaire barged into my office and straightened my ass out. I would have missed my opportunity with Tasha and my unborn child.

Chapter Fourteen

Zaire

"So, what brings you in, Mr. Price? It's been a few years since I have seen you," my therapist asked.

"Yeah, it has been a minute since I've been here, and it feels kinda weird."

"Okay, so what brings you here?"

"I'm about to get married. I love her so much, and I'm here because I need your advice. I need to know if I should tell my future wife about my past before we get married."

"What do you think you should do? Do you think that telling her will help her or hurt her more?"

"I don't know. That's why I'm here seeking advice. I love her so much and I don't want to walk into my marriage starting with a lie. But the other part of me is afraid to tell her because she's a rape victim and I don't want to set her back. She completed a great deal of therapy to get past it."

"That's a tough decision to make. I don't know who the lucky lady is, but I know you well enough to know that what you did was a big mistake and that you're not that type of person. So, I hope I'm not about to tell you the wrong thing. But honestly, I think you should keep it to yourself, and if she's a rape victim and you tell her that now, you will destroy her. Not only will she not marry you, she will never trust another man as long as she lives," my therapist told me.

"Thanks, Doc. I really appreciate this and everything that you have helped me work through."

"No problem. That's my job and congratulations, Mr. Price."

When I left my therapist, I went home, sat on my bed, and prayed to God that I was making the right decision by keeping my secret away from Nyla. When I was a young boy, I made a stupid decision hanging out with the wrong crowd. I ended up doing something really stupid that caused me to go to therapy because I couldn't live with what I did. It wasn't me, but that's what happens when you're a good guy trying to be bad. Once I gathered my thoughts, I knew I would only cause more hurt and damage if I said something, so I decided to take my therapist's advice. I was taking that shit to my grave. Somebody banging on my door brought me from my thoughts, and I wondered who the hell was at my door. I snatched my door open, and it was Cameron.

"Wassup? I'm surprised to see you here," I said to my brother.

"Look, I just needed someone to talk to, and you know I don't fuck with nobody. You were right about everything that you said to me this morning. I have been acting like an ass. I'm angry as fuck about all this new shit that we're finding out. I honestly don't know how you walk around like none of this shit happened."

"Man, I wasn't trying to make you feel bad. Someone just needed to check your stubborn ass, and since I'm the only one that can get that off, I figured I'll tell you what everyone is thinking but too afraid to say it to you."

"Well, thanks because I needed to hear it. But listen, you gonna be an uncle, nigga. When you left, I hopped in my car and googled the nearest abortion clinic," Cameron stated. I was looking at his ass like he was crazy. But I couldn't wait to hear the rest of the story.

"Then what happened, nigga? Just paused in the middle of a sentence like that," I said jokingly but was serious at the same time.

"I poured my damn heart out in front of your woman and every other nosey ass woman that was in the clinic. And at first, Tasha wasn't trying to hear shit I was trying to say. Man, when the nurse called her to the back, and she still went after everything that I had said to her, that shit crushed a nigga's soul. But then she came back out, now we're having a baby, and we're in a relationship," Cameron told me.

"Yo, I can't believe what the fuck I'm hearing right now. I mean, don't get me wrong; I'm happy for you. But I can't believe that you said you poured your heart out to a female and you're in a relationship," I told Cameron while laughing.

"Nigga, what the fuck is funny?" He asked, but before I got to answer, there was a knock at my door. When I opened the door, I was surprised to see Brian standing there. It's not that I had any beef with him, but shit was a little awkward after we found out that nigga was our brother and our cousin.

"Hey, Brian. Wassup?" I asked, stepping aside to let him in.

"Wassup, y'all? I'm glad that both of y'all are here because I need to get some shit off my chest. I know that finding out that we're biological brothers fucked y'all head up, but did either of you think about how that shit made me feel? We all grew up as brothers, and as soon as that horrible secret came out that destroyed the entire family, both of y'all turned y'all backs on me like I never meant shit to y'all. I would have never done that shit to the two of you. In fact, I needed you more now than I've ever had," Brian vented.

"You're right. We shouldn't have taken that shit out on you. I'm sorry, man," I apologized from my heart. I guess Cameron wasn't the only one being an ass.

"Yeah, me too, man. I'm sorry we shouldn't have let that shit separate us. We're so much better than that," Cameron chimed in. The three of us shared a hug and took a seat on the couch after pouring ourselves a drink. I guess this was the day for everyone to get their asses handed to them. But I was glad that we all made up so we could get past this shit and move forward. My phone ringing brought me from my thoughts. I knew it had to be Nyla because she told me she would call me when she got back in from hanging out with her sister. They were doing some last-minute shopping for the trip. I excused myself from my brothers to take my Chocolate Drop's phone call.

"Hey, baby. What you doing?" Nyla asked sexily into the phone.

"Sitting at home talking to my brothers. How was shopping with your sister?" I asked.

"I just got in. I'm tired, so I'm probably about to go to bed soon. I don't want to keep you from your brothers, so I'll talk to you tomorrow. I love you, Zaire,"

"You sure you don't want to talk a little longer? Those niggas can wait, no one comes before you," I assured Nyla.

"Aww, Zaire, you're so freaking sweet. I can't wait to be Mrs. Price," Nyla cooed into the phone.

"I can't wait to make you Mrs. Price. I love you, Nyla. Good night, baby."

"*Good night, Zaire.*" *After I hung up with Nyla, I went back to the living room and chatted with my brothers for a minute before the three of us decided to call it a night. Besides, I was tired, and I had a long day at the studio tomorrow.*

Chapter Fifteen

Tasha

"Mmm," I moaned softly as Cameron softly licked my soft, warm, pink center. I threw my head back and rested my head on the cabinet while I gripped the side sides of his counter. My legs were rested around Cameron's neck. Cameron's tongue moved faster on my clit, causing my slippery wet vagina to pulsate at a fast pace. I know I was close to climaxing inside of Cameron's warm mouth. Cameron inserted two fingers into my wetness and played inside my dripping pussy as if it was his playground.

"Cum for me!" Cameron demanded, and on que, my body obeyed his command. My body began to convulse as my muscles contracted.

"Ahh! Fuck, Cameron!" I yelled out in ecstasy. Cameron got up from his knees, slid his thickness into my wetness, and pumped in and out of me at a slow pace. I slowly gyrated my hips to match his pace. My legs were wrapped firmly around Cameron's waist as he thrust in and out of me.

"Damn, this pussy is good. You about to make me cum," Cameron groaned in my ear. As Cameron's strokes became faster and harder, my muscles tightened around Cameron's thickness. I yelled out in pure pleasure as I creamed on Cameron's dick.

"Fuck, Tasha! I'm about to bust," Cameron groaned while shooting his load inside of me. After catching our breath, Cameron helped me down off the counter.

"Damn babe, your pussy was already good, but this pregnant pussy is even better," Cameron stated while placing a kiss my lips. I just smiled as I walked off to clean myself up.

I had to hurry up and get dressed for my doctor's appointment. I couldn't believe that I was about to be a mother. At first, when Cameron showed up at the abortion clinic, I was pissed. When I got to the back, and they started asking me a bunch of questions and asking was I sure, I broke down. Cameron showing up begging for me not to go through with the abortion played a major part of me changing my mind. Although it's only been a few days, things were great with the two of us. Cameron refused to let me out of his sight, and I was loving every moment of it. I was now fully dressed and just waiting on my slow ass boyfriend to finish getting dressed. Cameron took longer than I did, so that saying about woman take forever was a total lie. Cameron had finally brought his ass downstairs, and when I looked up at him, I was ready to skip the doctor's appointment and ride that nigga's dick for the rest of the day.

"Damn, you like what you see?" Cameron's conceited ass asked.

"Boy, ain't nobody checking for your conceited ass. Let's get out of here before we be late to the appointment," I told him while putting on my coat. Cameron just gave me a yeah okay look before we headed out the door.

When we got to the doctor's, it was super packed, and I knew that I would be there for minute. I walked up to the front and signed in before sitting down. I looked up and noticed a few thirsty bitches starring at Cameron, so I decided to be petty and nastily kiss my man like it was just the two of us. I could hear a few women mumbling under their breath, but I didn't care.

"If you keep kissing me like that, I'm gonna take your ass in that bathroom and give you some act right," Cameron warned. I knew his ass wasn't playing, so I broke the kiss immediately. The receptionist called me to the desk to hand me a packet to fill out, and that shit was thick as hell. I filled the paperwork out then we went to the back. The nurse that came out to get us was about to make me smack the shit out of her ass. That bitch was acting like she didn't see me standing there with Cameron.

"Hi, I'm nurse Karen, and I'll be the nurse assisting Dr. Brad this morning," the nurse introduced herself but staring Cameron in the face like he was the patient. My patience was running thin with these thirsty bitches.

"Hello, Nurse Karen. I would appreciate it if you addressed me when you talked and not my man. I'm the patient," I snapped. Her mouth dropped open with embarrassment written all over her face.

"I'm sorry. I didn't mean any harm," Nurse Karen replied.

"Yeah, I bet. Can we get on with the visit?" I shot back sarcastically. Cameron chuckled and I nudged his arm.

The visit was finally over, and I was starving. I couldn't wait to go get something to eat. We pulled up to Bahama breeze for their happy hour, half-off appetizers. I was about to fuck up some Bang Bang shrimp and a few other things from the menu. Cameron had been kinda quiet since we left the doctors.

"Hey, is everything okay?" I asked, trying to figure out what was on his mind.

"Yeah, I'm good." Was the only thing that he said to me. I knew then that something was really bothering him.

"Cameron, I know that you're lying, so what's the problem? We were good."

"The doctor said that you were almost eight months. For one, your stomach is too flat to be almost eight months, but the bigger problem is that ain't my baby," Cameron stated seriously. I laughed so hard at his ridiculous yet funny statement. "What the fuck is so funny, Tasha?" Cameron asked, but I couldn't stop laughing.

"Boy, I'm laughing at your simple ass. The doctor said that I would be eight weeks next month, not eight months. Cameron, I can't believe you thought he said I was eight months. But all jokes aside, even if he did say that, why the hell wouldn't you have said anything? What were you gonna do, bail out on me again?" I asked seriously.

"Look, I'm sorry, Tasha. I should have been paying better attention, and shutting the world out is all I know how to do. I know it's not good for me, but it's all I know."

"Maybe you should go talk to somebody and get some professional help. That can help you find what the root of your issue is," I suggested.

"Nah, I'm good on that, but thanks for trying to help."

"Cameron, we're about to have a baby together, and I don't want you to do that to our child when things get rough. I also don't want them to think that's okay. I'm a big believer in communicating."

"I'll try to do better," Cameron replied while kissing the back of my hand. I knew that was his way of ending the conversation, so I decided to let it go for now.

"Look, when we leave here, there is someone I want you to meet."

"Okay," I replied, shoving the last bite of my food in my mouth. After Cameron paid for our meals, we headed out of the restaurant. Camron opened my car door for me before walking around to the driver's side. He got in and put his seatbelt on then peeled off. We were now at the Philadelphia bridge, and I was curious to where we were headed.

"Babe, where are we headed?" I asked.

"I'm taking you to meet my mom," Cameron answered. For some reason, I became extremely nervous at the thought of meeting Cameron's mom. I looked down at my clothes trying to make sure that I looked presentable. "Tasha, relax. You look great, Cameron stated. I guess he could tell that I was nervous.

"I'm just a little nervous," I told him honestly.

"Don't be. You'll be just fine." I just smiled and started playing with my fingers.

"So, tell me about your mom."

"It's not much to tell. One day she seemed to have it all together, and next thing I knew, she was strung out on drugs. We ended up losing our house and me and Zaire ended up living with my mom's sister and her husband. About a month ago, we found out that our uncle was really our dad," Cameron said nonchalantly. The car fell silent because I wasn't sure how to respond to what he had just told me.

"So, did she stop doing drugs?" I finally asked.

"I think so, either that or she slowed down. I just know that she's been doing much better," he replied while parking the car. I looked around the apartment complex, and we were sure enough in the projects of Philadelphia. As we walked to his mom's apartment building, I could see the drug boys outside dealing.

The closer we got to the door, the more nervous I became. Cameron grabbed my hand, and that gave me a little sense of comfort. When we got to the door, Cameron knocked on the door. When the door opened, I wasn't expecting her to look the way she did. Cameron's mom was a really nice-looking woman and didn't look like a crackhead at all. She even had nice long hair.

"Hey, baby. I'm surprised to see you here. Who's this beautiful woman you have here on your arm?" Cameron's mom asked while letting us in the door.

"Hey, mom. This is my girlfriend, Tasha. Tasha, this is my mom Candace."

"Hi, Ms. Candace. It's nice to meet you," I stated while holding my hand out for her to shake.

"It's a pleasure to meet you as well, but I don't do handshakes, I do hugs," she stated while hugging me. Y'all come on in here so we can get acquainted," Ms. Candance stated.

"You must be pretty special because you're the first girlfriend I've ever heard of. I mean, don't get me wrong; he's had plenty of hoes, but this girlfriend shit is new." Ms. Candance's statement caused me to blush.

"Well, Mom, I figured now was a good time for y'all to meet, since you would have me at her at the wedding in a few days. This is Nyla's best friend," Cameron told her.

"Well damn, y'all boys did well for yourselves. I wish you would have told me you were coming. I would've cooked something."

"We actually just came from eating, and I'm stuffed," I stated.

"Hey. What's up, Cameron?" I heard a man's voice say and for some reason, my breathing sped up, and I wasn't sure why. I looked up at him and just stared at the man. I wasn't sure why this man had that kind of effect on me, but I was suddenly uncomfortable.

"You good, baby?" Cameron asked. I just nodded my head, but I honestly wasn't okay. I felt like I was having a heart attack, but I didn't know why. From looking at him, he didn't look familiar, but it was something familiar about his voice.

"Can I use your bathroom?" I asked.

"Sure, baby. Let me show you where it is." Ms. Candance walked me over to the bathroom. When I closed the door, I tried to control my breathing, I turned on the water and splashed water on my face.

"Is she okay?" I heard Ms. Candace ask.

"Yeah, it may be the baby or something," Cameron stated.

"Oh my God, she's pregnant? Congratulations, baby. I can't believe I'm gonna be a grandma."

"My bad, mom. I didn't mean for you to find out this way."

After getting myself together, I finally walked back out. "Cameron, I'm not feeling to well can we go I need to lay down for a few."

Cameron and I stayed for a few more minutes just long enough to say our goodbyes before we left his momma's house. The ride home was kinda quiet. Cameron drove to his place, and as soon as we got in the door, I headed straight to his bedroom and laid down.

"Baby, what the hell was that about at my mom's house when her boyfriend came out? Do you know him or something?"

"Honestly, I don't know him. It was something about his voice that sounded familiar, but I can't remember from where. Look, I don't want to talk about it. It was crazy because I don't even know that man. But on another note, your mother is beautiful, and I can see where you get that smart-ass mouth of yours from," I told Cameron honestly.

"Yeah, my mom has always been beautiful, then she let the drugs take over, but even then, she was still pretty. She just didn't keep herself as much. Tasha, how come you never talk about your parents?" Cameron asked, catching me off guard.

I honestly didn't want to talk about my family because it wasn't much to talk about. I pretty much hated my mom, and I had no idea who my father was. Because my mother was a fucking whore.

"There isn't much to tell. My mom was a whore, I have no idea who my father is, and I don't have any siblings that I know of. I haven't seen or heard from my mother in about ten years, which was the day I ran away. Nyla's parents took me in and treated me as their own. The crazy thing was my mom never fought for me; she said I was better off with them. But soon after I moved in with Nyla, her parents died, but her brother Brandon still let me live with them. So, there you have it, that's all I have to say about my family. In a nutshell, Nyla and her family is the only family I have. Now baby, I need to take a nap. I'm really tired."

"Wow, I'm so sorry. I made you relive that, let's take a nap," Cameron replied then kissed me on the forehead. We both laid down, Cameron wrapped his arm around me and we both drifted off to sleep.

Chapter Sixteen

Candance

"Brad, you need to make up your mind. How in one sentence you're telling me how much you like me but can't be with me because I'm too young? But in the next sentence, you're trying to get in my pants. Fifteen is fifteen, so if I'm old enough for you to fuck me, then I'm old enough for us to be in a relationship," I said to Brad.

"I don't know how many times I have to tell your little ass that you cute and all, but I'm not going to jail for your lil' ass. You're only fifteen, and I'm about to turn twenty-one. I can't bring you out to no restaurants, but I promise in three years when you turn eighteen, we'll go wherever you want as much as you want. But for now, we have to keep this our little secret, "Brad stated.

I sat there on the side of the bed with my arms crossed, not believing a damn word he was saying. Brad was a block boy, and I knew he had another woman lined up. I knew I was too young for Brad, but he always made sure I was good and kept money in my pocket. My mom never realized that I was dressing different or that I was in love with a grown ass man because she was too busy with a needle in her arm. My sister Patricia and I use to be close until she left me with my drug-addicted mother and moved in with her best friend when she turned sixteen. Patricia was three years older than I was, but she could no longer deal with my mom's drug habit. I didn't have a best friend to move in with, so I stayed at home and raised my damn self.

"Candy, please don't start this pouting shit. I already told you what it was from the beginning. Now I know you didn't make me waste my damn money on this room. I told you that I love you and soon as you turn eighteen, it's gonna be me and you. We gonna travel the world," Brad said to me. I heard what Brad was saying. I just didn't believe him.

Brad walked over to the side of the bed that I was sitting on, stood in front of me, claimed on top of me and started kissing me. As mad as I was at him, I still kissed him back. Eventually, I stopped being mad and enjoyed the kiss and his hand roaming all over my body. I started to panic when he started unfastening my pants. As much as I liked Brad, I just wasn't ready to lose my virginity, especially to a guy that I couldn't even call my boyfriend in public.

"Brad, I'm not ready to cross that line with you. You know I'm still a virgin, and I want my first time to be special," I told Brad in between kisses.

"It will be special any and everything, and everything that we do together will be special." Brad just continued undoing my pants, and I kept telling him to stop, but for some reason, the more I said no, the more he heard yes. He just kept telling me to stop panicking and acting like a child because it was gonna feel good and make me a woman. I tried fighting him off, but it didn't work. Before I knew it, I felt a sharp pain in my virgin vagina. At that point, I laid there silently as the tears rolled down my face.

Brad just pretended not to see the tears or the fact that I wasn't enjoying what he was doing. He was talking and acting as if I was a willing participant. I couldn't believe that the man I felt like I was in love with, was having sex with me against my will, then had the nerve to want to me to enjoy it. Once the nightmare was over, he rolled over on the other side of the bed to catch his breath. I just laid there crying, never even looking at Brad. I felt so dirty and disgusting.

"You wanna order some room service? A nigga hungry as hell. And man, you got some good pussy."

"How can you just talk and ask me if I want to eat after you just raped me, Brad? I cried.

"What the fuck did you just say to me?" Brad yelled angrily, scaring the shit out of me. I didn't know if I should repeat what I said or not, but I was never the type to hold my tongue.

"Brad, you just fucking raped me, and now you acting like shit is good?" Before I could get the last word out, Brad slapped me so fucking hard that I thought he knocked my tooth out.

"Bitch, have you lost your fucking mind? If you ever say some dumb shit like that again, I'll kill your dumb ass. Get up and get dressed. I'm taking your ass home before I kill your stupid ass!" Brad threatened.

I jumped up so quick and got dressed. Before I could be fully dressed, that bastard was on the phone calling me a cab. I didn't bother saying shit because I couldn't wait to get away from his ass. "Candy, don't bother to call me. I'll reach out to you when I'm ready to deal with you," he had the nerve to say.

When I got home, all could do was cry. My mom was somewhere in her room getting high and fucking. She must have had company because she had music blasting. That was her norm when she had company over. I tried to call Patricia, but she didn't answer. I left several messages and she still didn't call me back. I honestly believe that if she would have returned my call, things wouldn't have gotten so out of hand with Brad. If she would have answered, I planned to tell her what Brad had done to me.

Two weeks went by, and I still hadn't heard anything from Brad. I was glad because at that point, I hated him. Or so I thought. I was walking home from school when I heard a horn blowing. When I turned around, it was Brad and his best friend Tim.

"Yo, meet me at the spot around six. We need to talk and take this money for a cab," he stated while passing me fifty dollars. I didn't say anything. I just put the money in my back pocket and kept it moving. I was surprised he said anything to me with Tim in the car. When I got in the house, I did my homework then took a shower and got dressed. The one thing I didn't play about was school. Even though my mom didn't give a damn if I went or didn't go, I still went faithfully every day.

"Hey, girl. Is you okay over there?" My friend, Tonya, asked, breaking me from my thoughts of me and Brad. I met Tonya at my drug program, we hit it off rather good, and we've been hanging out damn near every night.

"Yeah, girl, I'm fine. Was just thinking about my sorry ass baby dad and how he ruined my damn life," I admitted honestly.

"Girl, don't let that nigga have that kind of power. We're trying to get past all of that and leave his ass where his ass is at. He sounds like a piece of shit if you ask me. But I do think you need to talk to your sister. She's innocent in all of this," Tonya said. I knew she was right.

I did plan to reach out and talk to my sister before I went away to watch my son get married.

My name is Candance Price, I'm forty-five years old, and I was born and raised in Philadelphia. My childhood wasn't exactly anything to brag about. My mother was never really a mother to me and my sister. I ended up having my first kid at the age of sixteen and had to hide who the father was from the world because he was too old for me and wanted to keep me a secret. Even with me being a teenage mother of two kids through the grace of God, I still managed to finish high school and then landed a decent job. My life was going okay under the circumstances until I got hooked on drugs and lost everything, including my kids. As much as I loved my boys at the time, I loved the drugs more. But my boys are also the ones who made me want to get better and do better. Some may say it's too late since both of my boys are grown, but I say it's never too late to get it right.

I sat and talked with Tanya a little longer before I decided to call my sister to ask if we could meet. She had called me a few times, but I wasn't ready to talk.

Surprisingly, she answered on the first ring, and we agreed to meet up in the morning.

★★★★★

Patricia was on her way over here so we could talk. I decided to make the two of us some breakfast, and everything was just about done. I went and slipped on my clothes once the eggs were done. As soon as I slipped my shirt over my head, I heard the door. I instantly became nervous, but I told myself everything was gonna be okay. When I opened the door, I took in the beauty of my sister; she has always been breathtaking. I wasn't sure about anything else my mother was good for, but she damn sure made some beautiful daughters.

"Hello, Patricia," I spoke shyly.

"Hey, Candace. How are you?" Patricia spoke as she walked in the house.

"I'm pretty good. I made us some breakfast," I replied. We walked to the kitchen and I fixed our plates. I sat down, and both of us started eating in silence for a few moments before Patricia broke the silence.

"Look, Candance, I know this is hard, and I have no idea where to begin. I'm in the dark about all of this, but I think it's time that you catch me up to speed. And please don't spare my feelings," she stated, then took a sip of her orange juice. I swallowed the lump that was in my throat before speaking. I had completely lost my appetite at this point and hated that I had to travel down that lane that I tried so hard to forget about.

"I hate that part of my life, but I'm just gonna get straight to the point. Brad and I started talking not too long after you moved out. But because he was a little older than me, I had to keep us a secret, but I didn't want to. He used to always tell me that I couldn't say anything about us until I was eighteen. Anyway, we used to meet at the hotel to chill. He would give me money and buy me things. We weren't having sex; he wanted to, but I wanted to wait until we were official. But I guess he was tired of waiting for me. So, this particular day we were at the hotel, and we were arguing about sex. I told him if I was too young for us to be a couple, then I was too young to have sex with him, but he wasn't trying to hear that, so he took it. No matter how hard I cried and said no, the more he heard yes," I told her with tears in my eyes.

"Long story short, that was the day I lost my virginity, which was the worse day of my life. After he raped me, I confronted him about what he did, and he smacked the shit out of me then sent me home in a cab. When I got home, I cried for hours and tried calling you over and over again, but you wouldn't answer," I sobbed. The only thing that could be heard throughout the kitchen were sniffles between both of us.

"I'm so sorry, Candace. I should have never left you with Momma, then none of this would have happened. I felt bad every day, and when you got hooked on drugs, I tried to do right by the boys to make up for leaving you," Patricia cried. "How did you end up having two kids by him?" Patricia suddenly asked.

"Honestly being stupid, alone, and afraid. A couple of weeks after he raped me, he had me meet him at the hotel. When I got there, he had candles lit and music playing with a nice dinner set up. Brad apologized for what he did and told me it would never happen again and that he loved me and wanted us to be together. I was the one crazy enough to believe him. I mean, he did start treating me nice and doing a little more with me. I wasn't ready to have sex with him after what he did, but then I ended up finding out that I was pregnant with Cameron. I wanted to get an abortion, but for some reason, Brad wasn't having it. So, I decided to keep the baby but had to promise not to tell anyone that he was the father because he could go to jail.

When I was about six months, I left momma's house and moved into my apartment that Brad had gotten for me. So, we were good as far as I knew. We had two sons, and I still went to school and graduated because Brad made sure I didn't drop out. But all that shit changed when he came to the house one day and told me he couldn't be with me anymore. He told me that he's been messing with someone else, and she was about to have his baby. I felt like my heart had stopped, and all I could do was stare into space until I snapped out of it and started crying.

"Brad, what the fuck are you talking about? We have a family!" I cried.

"Look, Candy, I'll still take care of my kids. I love you, but I'm not in love with you. I'm in love with her."

I was so heartbroken because he wouldn't even talk to me. He just said what he said and bounced.

"And just like that, we were over. He would only come to see the boys and drop off money. Eventually, I became content with us not being together and just focused on me, Cameron, Zaire, and going to school. Anyway, a few months later, that's when you called and told me you were pregnant and getting married. I was really happy for you until I found out that you were with Brad and it crushed my soul. When I confronted him, he said that he didn't know you were my sister, but it was too late, and if I ever told you, he would kill me. I picked up the phone to call you, and he beat me like a nigga in the street to prove a point.

So as time went on, it ate me alive, and I started getting high. It was helping me cope at first, and I was doing it here and there. Then as time went on, I let it get the best of me and lost my job, house and kids. Brad stopped helping me then told me y'all were gonna raise my boys. So, there you have it, the story of me and Brad in a nutshell," I cried out. Patricia and I were both sobbing on one another.

"Candace, you should have told me. How could you let me have a baby and let me marry the father of your kids, on top of knowing that he was a piece of shit? I'm sorry that I left the way I did. And I'm even more sorry that I took it out on you. I just wanted to forget about that entire part of my past. I know that some of what happened to you was my fault because I wasn't there, but I was just trying to survive. I'm surprised you lost your virginity that way and not to one of momma's tricks. That's why I left, Candace. Momma let one of her tricks have sex with me for money. I hate that woman. She let a man take my innocence for some money for drugs. She was supposed to protect us from those things, not get paid to let it happen," Patricia cried.

Hearing my sister's story made me sick to my stomach, and now I understood why she left. I just wished she would have taken me with her. We cried and talked for a few more hours, playing catch up. I had to admit that it felt good, and I prayed that this wasn't our last time doing this. I was glad to hear that she put Brad out; she also told me that she filed for a divorce. I guess we'll have more time when we go to Zaire's wedding. I was also glad to hear that Cameron and Zaire finally reached out to her. Zaire is a lot easier to talk to, but that damn Cameron is the damn devil sometimes.

I guess he picked that trait up from Brad. After Patricia left, I put my dinner on to get ready for Charles to come over. I met Charles leaving from my program. He works in the building that my rehab is in, but he works in a different department. One day we started talking, and we really hit it off. Charles drives me to do great things, and he doesn't judge me for my past. He makes it easy to love him. I start working an office job the week I get back from the wedding. Charles put in a recommendation; I haven't even told the boys yet.

★★★★★

"Thanks for dinner, baby. That was delicious. Now let's take this shit to the bedroom so I can have my dessert," Charles flirted. I didn't hesitate to take my ass to the bedroom because Charles had some great dick. I was having the best sex of my life with Charles. He was fifty years old, but you would never know it if he didn't tell you his age. He lived in the gym and had a body to die for. As soon as we got into the bedroom, Charles didn't waste any time stripping me out of my clothes and exploring my body. As soon as Charles' big hands roamed my body, I felt my juices flowing. I let out a soft moan.

"Damn, this pussy wet already just like I like it," Charles stated before diving into my wetness with his mouth. Charles and I spent the next hour exploring each other's bodies, making one another cum over and over again.

Chapter Seventeen

Cameron

"Tasha, your ass ain't done packing yet?" I yelled upstairs.

"I'm almost finished. You know I have to make sure I have everything," she yelled back. I walked up the steps to see what her ass was up there doing. When I got up there, I saw two suitcases and a carry-on. I just shook my head.

"Tasha, where the hell do you think you going with all this shit? We only gonna be gone for five days," I asked.

"Babe, this is just what woman do. You can never overpack too much, and did you forget my best friend is getting married in two days?"

"Girl, bring your ass. We gotta go. You know we have to get up early to catch this flight, and we still haven't even eaten dinner yet," I told Tasha's ass. '

We'll be here all damn night waiting on her slow ass. She just rolled her eyes while I carried her heavy ass luggage downstairs. If her ass weren't pregnant, I would have made her carry her own shit. After getting all of her shit in the car, I drove off and headed over the bridge to my house. When we pulled up, we got out the car.

"Well, it's about time you got home," I heard a female's voice say. I turned around, and it was some chick I fucked once like damn near a year ago. I don't even know how that bitch knew where I lived.

"What the fuck are you doing at my house?" I snapped.

"I thought that you might want to know that I was about to have your baby," she stated, and all I could do was laugh because I knew that bitch was lying. Tasha looked at me with wide eyes and I knew I had to dead that shit Asap. I just got with Tasha; I wasn't about to lose her already.

"Baby, this bitch is a liar. Let me handle this, but you stay right here," I assured Tasha. I wasn't worried about this being true, not even a little bit. She was about to regret popping up to my fucking house with this bullshit.

"Yo, I don't know what the fuck went through your mind that gave you the balls to pop up at my fucking house with this shit, but what I do know is you better get your hoe ass from in front of my door. I fucked your hoe ass once, and I was double strapped when we did it. And secondly, if your hoe ass is so pregnant, lift your shirt up," I told her. Both Tasha and Brittany both looked at me like I was crazy, and I guess Tasha caught on because she started laughing.

"What the fuck is so funny, bitch?" Brittany snapped.

"Bitch, I'm laughing at your thirsty ass and your lop-sided stomach," Tasha replied, and we both laughed at her dumb ass. She looked down at her stomach then tried to rush Tasha, but Tasha was quick and dragged her before I could stop her. I broke up the fight because if something happened to my baby, I was going to kill that bitch.

As I pulled Tasha off Brittany, her fake stomach she had attached to her was falling off. I couldn't do shit but shake my head. Of course, she was popping hella shit, and I was trying to hold Tasha back.

"Tasha, chill the fuck out because if something happens to my baby, I'm gonna kill some fucking body," I yelled, holding her back. "Brittany, I don't know what the fuck your problem is, but you need to leave and don't ever come back to my house ever again in life."

"Fuck you, Cameron. If you think you can just treat me like some hoe, you got the game fucked up. You, bitch, are gonna regret the day you put your hands on me," Brittany threatened before hopping in her car and peeling off. I made sure to remember her license plate number because that bitch had to be dealt with immediately. Tasha and I both walked into the house, and no sooner than the door shut, Tasha went at it.

"Cameron, who the fuck was that crazy bitch? I'm out here fighting a bitch I don't even know while being pregnant?" Tasha yelled angrily.

"Tasha, calm down. I know that was some crazy shit that just happened, but she will get dealt with when we get back. I fucked that girl once and haven't seen or heard from her since. I don't even know how that bitch knew where I live," I explained honestly.

"Please get your hoes in order because I'm not into fighting bitches over a nigga that supposed to be mine. But anyway, I'm done with this conversation. What are we going to eat?" She stated, changing the subject. For some reason, she just made me love her even more. I guess I liked my woman a little spicy.

"What do you have a taste for?" I asked.

"I guess we can order Chinese," she replied. I found the menu, and we ordered Chinese and chilled for the rest of the night. We watched a movie and then got it in before going to sleep. We had a long day ahead of us.

Chapter Eighteen

Nyla

I couldn't believe I was getting married in a couple of days this shit just seemed unreal to me, but I was super excited. I was on my way to pick Ariel up so we could do some last-minute shopping so we could pack and get ready to leave in the morning. I knew I was over packed, and I knew when Zaire saw how much shit I was taking that he was going to have a fit. I had Keisha Cole's Cd blasting through the car as I drove to my sister's house. When I pulled up, I didn't even bother to get out I just sent her a text letting her know I was outside. Ariel walked outside smiling looking beautiful as usual. I had to admit, my siblings and I weren't bad looking at all.

"Bitch I didn't need you to text to let me know you were outside with that loud as music that was playing," Ariel stated while getting in the car.

"Whatever, anyway you look cute," I told her while pulling off.

"Thanks, you look cute yourself, she replied. I just smiled and turned the music back up and pulled off.

We pulled up to the mall in Twenty minutes, the first store I planned to hit was Victoria secret because I needed some sexy shit for my big night. For some reason I've been hornier than a mother fucker and Zaire refused to give in and give me some dick or any type of real four play. When we got in the store, I saw something that caught my eye immediately. I walked over to that rack and it was my size and I was happy as hell because it was the last one, they had. After buying a few more sets along with some new underwear and bras we finally made our way to the counter. I noticed Ariel had some lingerie in her hand and I looked at her with the side eye because I wondered who the hell, she was wearing that for with her single ass. After paying for our things we hit the Jewelry store then headed to buy some perfume. I could tell by the way my sister was acting and the things she was buying that she must have been seeing someone. But I wanted to see if she would tell me or would I have to ask because it wasn't like Arial to keep anything from me. once we were done our shopping, we decided to go grab something quick at the food court to hold us until dinner at Brandon's tonight. Zaire was going to head over after we go to see my therapist. I honestly think he would like her a lot. I only ordered a cheeseburger and a drink because I needed to save room for my pretzel.

"I have to tell you a secret," Ariel stated. I looked up at her as I took a bite of my burger. "I've been seeing someone for the past three months, but I didn't want to say anything until I seen where it was going. But I think we're getting pretty serious since we've been spending a lot of time together.

"Wow I knew something was up when I saw you buying lingerie. But I'm happy for you so when do we get to meet him?" I questioned excitedly.

"Well I was thinking at dinner tonight and it's her and her name Jasmine," Arial stated, and I spit my soda out across the table.

"Her? Are you serious? When the hell did you start liking pussy?" I blurted. Arial bust out laughing but I didn't see shit funny. Don't get the wrong impression I don't have anything against to women being together I just was shocked to hear that my sister was into women.

"I got into them three months ago, I mean I still like men, but I like her too. She's pretty, smart, she has her own shit and she's great in bed. I never had nobody eat my pussy like she do," she replied. I was ready to throw up.

"Come on Ariel that last part was so nasty don't nobody want to hear that shit," I told her.

"Keep that same energy when Zaire finally eat that shit and suck your soul, as soon as you try to tell me about it I'ma say the same shit, Ariel warned but I wasn't paying her ass no mind because as soon as I got back from my honeymoon I was going into every detail about my official first time.

"Girl by I'm telling you everything," I said as we both laughed. "But all jokes aside I can't wait to meet her. If you're happy then I'm happy but I can't wait to see the look on Brandon's face when you tell him you're a carpet muncher, I said laughing hard as hell at my own joke.

"Bitch your ass is so fucking goofy let's get out of here since I have a few more things to do before I head over to

Brandon's. After I dropped Ariel back off at home, I took my ass back home so I could pack the things I just brought so I wouldn't have anything to do when we got back from Brandon's. I was gonna put everything in Zaire's truck before we left since I was staying the night at Zaire's.

As soon as I got in the house, I put everything that I brought in my luggage. I neatly put my wedding dress away then got out something comfortable to wear on the plane tomorrow. Once I was done packing, I jumped in the shower and got dressed. On my way downstairs I heard the door open and I knew it had to be Zaire.

"Hey baby, I missed your chocolate ass, Zaire said placing his lips over mine. I deepened the kiss and as the kiss was coming to an end, I gently sucked his bottom lip.

"I missed you too baby, I told him. Can you go get my luggage from upstairs we need to go since we still have to stop pass my therapist first then get to Brandon's. I put everything by the door. Zaire walked up the steps and as soon as he reached my bedroom door all I heard was "What the fuck!" I just snickered to myself. Zaire walked downstairs with luggage in each hand.

"Damn babe what the hell did you pack all this for? You do plan on coming back home don't you?"

"You so silly, yes I'm coming back home. This isn't even a lot, but I have to make sure I have enough clothes plus my wedding dress and things.

"All this damn luggage I gotta pay for is gonna be near the price of the flight you could have left all this shit except the wedding dress", Zaire joked. "Besides after we say our vows and chill with the family for a little bit you not gonna need one damn thing out those bags. Your ass gonna have dick in you the entire trip. So, I hope your ass been making sure you're good with the birth control because I ain't pulling out," Zaire stated seriously. All I could do was blush at his comment. After making sure everything was locked up and my alarm was set, we headed out the door.

"Where did you say your therapist was located again? Zaire asked. I gave him the address that Dr. Bridgette gave me, and we pulled off. We pulled up in fifteen minutes and this building didn't look anything like the building I usually went to. We got out the car and walked up to her office. I knocked on the door and she yelled come in.

"Hi Dr. Bridgette, I can't stay long but this is my fiancé Zaire, Zaire this is my therapist Dr. Bridgette. She's the reason we're getting married," I stated excitedly. But for some odd reason I was the only one that seemed excited. The room had fell awkwardly silent.

"Well hello, it's finally nice to meet the man of the hour, I've heard so much about you. You have a great woman on your hands, and you seem like a great man, Dr. Bridgette finally spoke.

"Thank you I've heard a lot about you as well. I don't think we'll be getting married if it wasn't for you," Zaire replied while shaking Dr. Bridgette's hand. I wasn't sure if I was tripping or not but both Dr. Bridgette and Zaire seemed to be acting funny.

"So, are you ready for your big day?" Dr. Bridgette turned to ask me.

"Yes, I'm ready, a little nervous but I'm ready.

"There's no need to be nervous Chocolate Drop, I got you," Zaire assured. I just smiled at his comment.

"You'll be just fine Nyla, I don't mean to rush you out, but I have a client on the way in Dr. Bridgette stated.

"No worries we have to get going ourselves, I'll make an appointment to see once I get back and get settled.

"Okay, congratulations to you both."

"Thanks," we both said in unison. Zaire and I both left out of the office and I still felt really weird. Something wasn't right I just couldn't seem to put my finger on it. The ride to my brother's house was silent until I broke the silence

"So, is it me or was that visit a little weird?" I asked Zaire.

"I think it was just fine, baby you worry too much," Zaire stated.

"Yeah you're probably right."

"Hey, y'all just in time dinner just got done and Arial texted and said she'll be pulling up in three minutes and Mariah is in the kitchen.

I walked into the kitchen to go see Mariah her and I had become pretty close. I was glad that my brother was finally happy and found someone to settle down with.

Mariah was good for him and I wasn't worried about him being a good father because he was gonna be a great father.

"Hey boo," I spoke cheerfully.

"Hey sis, wassup you ready to get out of here in the morning?" Mariah asked.

"Hell, yeah I'm ready and are you sure that it's okay for you to fly?"

"Yup I reconfirmed this morning at my appointment, everything will be just fine. Nyla you're such a worrier."

"So, I've been told." We all was sitting at the table and in walked Ariel and Miss Jasmine.

"Hey fam, this is my Girlfriend Jasmine and Jasmine this my family. My sister Nyla and her fiancé Zaire, my brother Brandon, and his girlfriend Mariah.

"Define girlfriend," Brandon, inquired.

"She means girlfriend, as in the one that makes her cum numerous of times within minutes," The girl Jasmine answered, and I swear if y'all could see the look on everyone's face. I had to admit she was a beauty. And although she was blunt, I liked it.

"Ariel when the fuck did you become a lesbian? No offense to you Jasmine you're beautiful and obviously you have no filter, but I'm just a little caught off guard. Brandon asked.

"We can get into all that another time, I promise I'll tell y'all everything but for tonight let's just chill and eat, we have along ass day tomorrow," Ariel replied. After talking over dinner and getting to know Jasmine I actually liked her a lot so far. After dinner we all took a shot, then went our separate ways to get some rest.

Chapter Twenty

Zaire

Ever since me and Nyla left Dr. Bridgette's office I've been fucked up. How the fuck did we end up with the same therapist? I wasn't sure how I should move at this point. I knew I couldn't call off the wedding, but I was damn sure having doubts. That therapist know some of my darkest secrets that no one's besides the two of us know. I knew she couldn't disclose what I discuss with her, but I was still nervous as hell. Nyla and Dr. Bridgette seemed to be pretty close and Nyla was very fond of her to the point she wanted her to come to the wedding. I feel even worse pretending not to know who she was. Nyla is gonna be upset and feel like I'm hiding something if I don't tell her that I already knew Dr. Bridgette before tonight.

"Baby are you okay? You've been kind of quiet tonight." Nyla asked.

"Yeah baby everything is good over here just making sure that everything is straight for our big day," I answered.

"You not getting cold feet on me, are you?"

"Why would I get cold feet when I'm about to marry the woman of my dreams not to mention the most amazing woman I've ever met," I told Nyla while placing my lips over hers. I loved Nyla with everything in me I just hated keeping this deep secret from her, but I don't think she would understand, and I was sure if I told her I would lose her for sure. This was something that no one knew, and I wanted to keep it that way.

"I love you so much Zaire, I'm so glad that you stalked me at the movie theater," Nyla stated with a chuckle.

"So, is that what you're gonna tell our kids, that I stalked you?" I asked jokingly.

"Well it does have some truth to it."

"Tell them whatever you need to tell them to make your story work, you were all over a nigga the moment you saw this handsome face," I joked. "Come on babe let's get some sleep we have an early morning. And I love you too Nyla Price." After sharing a kiss, we took our asses to sleep.

✶✶✶✶✶

My alarm going off caused me to jump up I tapped Nyla letting her know it was time to get up and get going because I didn't want to miss our flight. We both got up handled our hygiene and threw something comfortable on and headed out the door. I threw on a tee-shirt and some sweatpants. When I looked up Nyla was wearing a pair of blue tights with a blue stripe shirt with a pair of blue and white low top chucks. Her hair was in a ponytail and even though was considered a basic look she looked super beautiful and natural to me. I just stared at my soon to be wife for a few moments taking in her beauty and shape and my baby was a baddie.

"I can't wait to make you my wife," I blurted.

"I can't wait to become your wife," Nyla replied. I just smiled and loaded my truck with my things since Nyla things were already in the truck. Before pulling off I texted Karee and Josh to let them know that I was leaving and make sure they do their daily rounds at the studio and my home. I hired them when I first got big in the music business. When we got to the airport, I was surprised to see that everyone was there except my Aunt Pat and Brian. My mom and her boyfriend Charles was even there already. We walked up spoke to everyone.

"He y'all wassup?" I spoke as Nyla gave out hugs, it was too damn early for me to be hugging people so wassup was all they were getting from a nigga. The only one I hugged was my momma and that shit was brief. A few moments later my Aunt Pat and Brian walked up. I looked around the room and smiled because I couldn't believe all the people, I loved the most was all here for my big day. I felt a little bad that Nyla's parents wouldn't get to see their daughter walked down the aisle, but I was grateful for Brandon stepping up and being there for his sisters. In some ways I wished I had a sister and in other ways I was glad that I didn't because I knew if a nigga did to my sister like me and Cameron use to do chicks, I'll be somewhere in jail for killing a nigga.

"Mr. Price your plane is ready your party can board the plane now," a woman said over the loudspeaker. I found that to be a little weird, but I looked over at Cameron and he was wearing a sneakily smirk on his face. Everybody started boarding the plane and I noticed that no one else was on the plane nor were there any assigned seats to anyone. I knew that Cameron Paid for everyone's ticket, so I never had a ticket in my hand.

"This is just one of my many surprises," Cameron walked up to me and said.

"Nigga did you rent the entire plane out?"

"Hell, yeah we gonna have so much fucking fun on this motherfucker. My little brother is getting married this shit only happens once and you deserve the best, on top of that I'm your fucking best man," Cameron stated happily bringing me in for a hug. I genuinely loved my brother and don't know where I would do without him.

"Thanks man this is some tv shit man, but I love you man and you don't know how much I appreciate you., I told Cameron honestly.

"No problem man but don't get all soft on a nigga, you ain't bout to make me cry, he replied. I didn't expect anything less from Cameron.

Everyone slept for the first two hours of the flight then after that we partied, ate and drunk for the entire flight. I can't remember ever having this much fun. We had three more hours left before we will be in Costa Rica. I looked around the room and everyone looked so happy. My mom and Charles looked good together and I was so glad that my mom had gotten herself together and was able to be here with us today. I planned to make it my business to get to know the man that my momma was dating because I didn't play about my mom and I wanted to make sure she he was who she thought he was. I was also happy to see my mom and my aunt Pat speaking and getting along.

*****

An hour before our flight landed, I heard my phone buzz indicating that I had a text message when I pulled my phone out, I looked down at my phone and it was a text from Karee.

Karee: Boss we had a problem at your crib we had to lay out two niggas at the crib well one was a female, but I swear we didn't know she was wearing a ski mask along

with the dude. *I had to reread that shit three times before I could respond.*

Me: What the fuck! Do you know who they are?

Karee: Boss I was hoping you didn't ask that. But it's Sharee from the record label and Mike from "We Get It Done Records" I had to read that text multiple times before that shit sunk in. I could feel the blood draining from my face I was so pissed.

Me: Are those motherfuckers dead?

Karee: Mike is dead for sure but Sharee is fighting for her life, the ambulance just took her out. But look I know this is fucking with you but don't let this ruin your trip. You're about to get married. Me and Josh got this shit over here, the detective may give you a call. I suggest you let it go to voicemail then call him back when you feel like talking or you can get away from Nyla.

Me: Yeah you right but I'm about to let Cameron and Brian know what's up. My flight about to land in less than an hour. Let me know if anything else come up.

After my last text I called Cameron and Brian to the back of the plane to tell them what was up. Cameron's crazy ass was ready to go back to the states and see what was up, but we knew that we couldn't. I decided to let that shit be until I got back home. I couldn't afford to worry about that shit right now.

Chapter Twenty-One

Nyla

We just got to Costa Rica and I couldn't believe how beautiful it was here, the water was clear blue not like the dirty ass water in the states, I was in heaven already. I thought we were saying at a hotel, but Cameron apparently cancelled the hotel reservations and rented us this big ass house that people like me could only dream of. There were so many rooms and the décor was beautiful in every room. I was in the shock of my life when I walked into me and Zaire's room. It was huge and romantic and away from everyone's else room which I loved.

"Oh my God! I love it here," I said in awe while covering my face.

"Yeah this room is fire, thanks bro I could never repay you for all you've done," Zaire said to Cameron.

"I have a few more surprises up my sleeve for the both of you. This is gonna be one vacation neither of you will forget, Cameron stated. I hugged Cameron tightly. I couldn't believe I was about to go from one brother to three brothers and just twenty-four hours. Zaire and I put our things away then found everyone else. The family wasted no time hitting the pool, I went and changed into my bathing suit and joined everyone else.

"Hey bestie this fucking house is insane, I would love to live in a house like this," Tasha said as soon as I got in the pool.

"Bitch who you telling, I love it here. But can you believe that I'm getting married tomorrow evening?"

"Actually, I can't believe it, but what I do know is you deserve this more than anyone. Zaire is a great guy and loves you very much, anybody can see that he loves you.

"Thanks girl, Zaire is great, a little too great if you ask me, the man is damn near perfect," I replied honestly.

"You just be ready for tonight events," Tasha said sneakily.

"Bitch tonight is our girl's night after eight o'clock tonight you won't see Zaire until tomorrow evening when you walk down that isle girl. I know you didn't think me, and Ariel wasn't gonna go all out for you. You deserve this shit Nyla and we gonna party hard this is your last night as a single woman, so you better get all you're twerking out tonight unless you twerking on the dick.

"Oh my God you are crazy girl. And speaking of Ariel that bitch has a girlfriend," I blurted. Tasha eyes got wide. She was just as shocked as I was.

"Yes, bitch her name is Jasmine I met her last night at Brandon's."

"Bitch I know you lying, Ariel eating pussy now? I'm shocked. Well is the girl at least cute or did she go get herself one of those butch looking bitches?" Tasha asked with her face ripped up. I couldn't do shit but laugh at Tasha because she was funny as hell. Tasha had absolutely no filter at all.

"Actually, she's very pretty with a nice ass body, I was shocked my damn self. But girl you should have seen Brandon's face when she told him that was her girlfriend."

"I could only imagine," Tasha chuckled.

For the next hour we had a fucking ball. Zaire dunked me in the water a few times not to mention the water gun fight guys against the girls. I was having an awesome time but unfortunately it was time to get out to have dinner. We had maids, butlers, and housekeepers in this bitch. I felt like I moved up to the rich life. Zaire and I didn't really talk about our finances, but I honestly didn't think him, and Cameron had that kind of money, but I guess I thought wrong. We sat down for dinner and I had no idea what the hell I was about to eat but it looked good as hell. It had rice, black beans, tortillas, salad beef, chicken and pork. We also had fresh fruit and some delicious looking fresh fruit juice. I couldn't wait to dig into all that food.

"Excuse me what is the name of this meal?" I asked the server.

"It's called Casado, it's one of the most popular dishes we serve here in Costa Rica.

"Thank you it looks delicious; I told the server. After Mr. Charles blessed the table, we all dug in. I couldn't believe how good the food was. We laughed and joked while eating until it was time to get for ready, for only God knows what we were about to get into.

"Can I have everyone's attention please?" Brandon stood up and said. For those who don't know I'm Nyla's brother Brandon, and she means the world to me. I am glad that she met Zaire and let him and love her the way a woman is supposed to be loved. With that being said Cameron and I have some very special things planned to make sure that Nyla and Zaire has the time of their life here in Costa Rica. I love you sis but I'm gonna have to steal him away from you tonight beings though this is his last night as a free and single man. I'll make sure he keeps it respectful but I'm also gonna make sure he has fun. I love you Nyla and I can't wait to see you in your dress tomorrow when I walk you down the aisle. Y'all have about a half hour to say or do whatever y'all need to do to hold y'all over until tomorrow evening," Brandon said bringing tears to my eyes.

"I love you too Brandon, and thanks for all you do for me I don't know where I would be today if it wasn't for you, I said Blowing him an air kiss. After Brandon's speech Zaire and I was headed to our room when someone rang the doorbell. We all looked around at one another and wondered who could be at the door.

"Is there an Ariel here? You have a house guest," the butler stated. A few seconds later Jasmine walked into the eating area. I was surprised to see her here.

"Oh my God! Jasmine what are you doing here? Wait how did you get here or know where I was located.

"Well your brother invited me last night when you went to the bathroom. He booked me a flight and told me to let him know when I landed so he could tell me what hotel y'all was at. But this right here is beautiful. I'm gonna have a lot of fun with you in this house," Jasmine stated with a wink. Ariel's face lit up like it Christmas day. She ran over and gave Jasmine a big hug and kiss then thanked Brandon.

★★★★★

Later that night the girls and I were dressed up and headed to God's know where. Nobody would tell me where we were going. Less than a half hour later we pulled up to this big building. As soon as we walked a half-dressed woman came and took us to our area. Once we were all seated the drinks started floating around, I knew not to drink too much because that just wasn't my thing. After the second drink "Back that ass up by Juvenile" came on and we all got up to shake our asses. To my surprise, my soon to be mother in-law had some pretty good moves.

"Now that you ladies are nice and tipsy let's get y'all some live entertainment, please ladies take a seat and enjoy the show." the DJ stated on the mic. The other woman started screaming like some groupies at a concert. "First up to the stage is Chocolate Thunder!" the DJ announced.

The song "Sex You" blared through the speakers, when I looked up, I spotted a big chocolate muscular dancer walking up. When he got to the middle of the floor where we were located, he begin his performance. I couldn't front if I wanted to his body was everything. And I loved the way he was moving. We started throwing ones at him and he started walking towards us and grabbed Jasmine out of her seat and took her to the middle of the floor. I was in awe with the way he was dancing with her and to my surprise she seemed to be enjoying it. Once he was finished with his performance another guy came out, he was on the brown skin side, but he was cute as well with a nice body. He came out to "Pony by Ginuwine" I couldn't believe how fun It was watching strippers. This was my first time, but I was truly enjoying myself.

"Now we have something a little special for Ms. Nyla. I hear she's tying the not tomorrow so we wanna make sure her last night as a single woman will be one, she'll never forget. All the way from mother fucking Philadelphia we have the prettiest light skinned nigga with the prettiest eyes. Bringing out none other than Mr. fucking Twilight," I looked up and my God this nigga was fine. But as he got closer my heart started beating faster because I was nervous and mesmerized at the same time. He came out off of "Grind on me, by Pretty Ricky." When he started walking towards me, I thought my heart was about to jump out of my chest it was beating so fast. Twilight grabbed my hand and led me to the middle of the floor. He grabbed a chair and sat me in it.

I was so glad that I didn't wear the dress I planned to wear because I would really be in trouble. I decided to wear a teal one-piece romper with a pair of silver rhinestone opened toed heels with silver accessories and my hair was in a high ponytail. The song switched to "Nothing On," by Tank's freaky ass. Twilight got on his knees and pretended to eat my pussy, but he really wasn't, but he definitely had me feeling some type of way down there. He stood me up and turned me around and grinded on my ass before lifting me up in the air. I let a loud squeal while covering my face. Everyone was laughing and screaming and cheering him on. I couldn't lie even though I was a little uncomfortable because it felt like I was cheating on Zaire, I was having the time of my life. After the performance was over, I thought the night was over, but boy was I wrong. We walked upstairs to a room full of dance poles and a dance instructor.

"Bitch are you ready for this? It's about to be so fucking lit!" Tasha yelled pulling my hand to follow her. They had outfits for us to change into which I thought was cool they said you could dance in heels or barefoot. I knew I was about to have so much fun.

Bitch yes thank y'all for this night I've never had this much fun in my life I stated as I changed into my skimpy shorts and tank top.

Chapter Twenty -Two

Zaire

I hated to leave my soon to be wife, but I was having so much fun once we left the house that I barely had any time to think about her plus I knew she was probably having just as much fun as I was. I was at some big ass palace that had some of the baddest fucking dancers you could fine. I had a bad ass private dancer named Aliz'e. I knew for sure that I loved Nyla after having something that looked that good and I wasn't even attempted to hit it if this was six months ago, I would have slid on a condom and fucked the shit out of her ass. I looked around and everyone was having just as much fun as I was. I was surprised to see Brandon as loose as he was with the dancers, beings though he was in a relationship and had a baby on the way, but my lips were sealed. Cameron had a bad bitch on his lap and surprisingly he was having fun yet behaving himself.

"Yeah bro I see you over there," Cameron yelled to me.

"I see you too bro." I scanned the room and didn't see Brian's ass nowhere in sight. That nigga was probably in a private room getting his dick sucked. Aliz'e got off my lap and grabbed the bottle of Aliz'e off table I thought she was finished until she laid on the floor and spread her legs as wide as they could go. She shook the bottle then inserted the bottle inside of her. My eyes damn near popped out of my head when she did that shit. She opened the bottle, and it oozed out of her all on and inside of her. That shit was sick, then she slowly pulled the bottle out and deep throated it. I was done at that point this was some shit you only seen white bitches do in porn.

"Got damn girl what the fuck," I said.

"Now you know why they call me Alize, she stated before walking off. She left my head spinning. That was some crazy shit. After a few more hours of partying we decided to call it a night. We headed back to the house and talked and fucked around for another couple of hours before calling it a night.

When I got to my room I stripped out of my clothes and got my drunk ass in the bed. As soon as I laid down, I instantly become lonely and was missing my Chocolate Drop like crazy. Not to mention I was horny as hell and couldn't wait until tomorrow so I could make love to my wife. I ain't had no pussy in months and I needed to get some, I was tired of beating off. I knew they said we couldn't see one another until tomorrow night but they ain't say shit about not talking to her. I grabbed my phone off the nightstand and sent a text first, I didn't want to stop her fun if she was still out.

Me: Hey baby are you still out?

Chocolate Drop: Hey baby I was just thinking about you. No, I just got in and got in the bed, I think I'm drunk. I want some dick Zaire, come make love to me baby. I had to reread that text twice, but the words didn't change. You have no idea how bad I wanted to take her up on her offer, and I was horny too.

Me: Babe you can't be texting shit like this as horny as I am. Do you know how long it's been since I had some? What are you trying to do, give me blue balls?

Chocolate Drop: Eww Blue balls is a real thing? I couldn't do shit but laugh at her text.

Me: They won't literally turn blue, but I can get so hard that it starts to hurt if I don't get none.

Chocolate Drop: Well you won't get blue balls if you come get this pussy, it's yours anyway. I bricked up immediately after reading that last text. Nyla had to be hella drunk to be talking this reckless. Before I could respond back, she called.

"Hey baby you over there talking really reckless, how much did you have to drink?"

"I had a few drinks but I'm so horny right now so are you coming to give me some Zaire?" she asked sexily. Nyla wasn't making this easy, but I had to stand my ground.

"I can't do that Nyla, but what we can do is have phone sex, we can video chat and I'll watch you and you can watch me."

"Oh my God, that's so nasty Zaire but I'm down, but you do know I don't know anything about no video phone sex so don't laugh at me if I get it wrong, Nyla stated.

"I got you baby, I'm about to hang up and video chat you," I told her. With that I hung up and video chatted with my Chocolate drop. Surprisingly, we had some good *phone sex. And once we were finished, It didn't take either of us long to fall asleep.*

Chapter Twenty-Three

Nyla

When I woke up the next morning my head was pounding so damn bad that I could barely get out of bed. When I finally sat up, I noticed that my panties were off and I started to panic, wondering how the hell did my panties get off. Everything was a blur from last night, I guess I had too much to drink. I slid my panties on and went to find the bathroom after handling my hygiene I went to find some pain killers. I knocked on Ariel's door and turned the knob and that was the biggest mistake ever. I felt like I had to throw up after seeing my sister eating pussy. "Oh my God," I said before quickly closing the door back. On my way back to my room I ran into Ms. Candace.

"Good morning Nyla, are you okay?" You look like you saw a ghost." Yes, I'm fine I just have a bad headache," I told her.

"Well let's get you something for that headache then get this day started, we have a long day ahead of us you're marrying my son in a few hours. After taking some Motrin we headed downstairs to have breakfast. When I got down there everyone was in attendance except Ariel and Jasmine but why would she be hungry she already had her breakfast. I went and sat at the table next to Tasha.

"Damn bitch you look like shit," Tasha whispered.

"I feel like shit, I have a headache but it's going away, my mother in law gave me some Motrin. But bitch how I walked in on Ariel eating pussy and now I'm disgusted," I told Tasha while shaking my head.

"Damn the morning just started and you sound like you're having a rough one already. You need some coffee you did drink a decent amount last night. We have to get you right for your big day."

"Tell me about the drinking I woke up with my panties down and I have no idea how they got off.

"Damn girl," Tasha snickered. After eating and drinking some coffee I was feeling a lot better. Ariel and Jasmine finally made their way to the table. She and I awkwardly looked at one another but not much was said.

*****

A few hours had now passed, and it was getting closer to one of the most important moments of my life and I was starting to get nervous. I was thinking of every reason why we shouldn't get married but I couldn't find anything that made sense.

"Hey Nyla, I'm sorry that you had to see that earlier, I should have made sure the door was locked," Ariel said breaking me from my thoughts.

"Hey there's no need to apologize I should have waited for an answer before coming in. I mean you are a grown woman in a relationship," I replied honestly.

"Let's just forget about it, so is my baby sister ready to get married?"

"I'm as ready as I'm gonna get, I mean I can't lie and say that I'm not nervous. I'm not nervous to get married I'm nervous about the honeymoon. What if I freak out when we have sex and get a flash back to the night I was raped? Zaire don't deserve that on our wedding night.

"I'm sorry to just walk in but I overheard what you said about being raped, if you don't mind can I share a story with you?" Ms. Candace asked, and I nodded my head yes.

"I'm not sure if Zaire told you or not but I was raped by Zaire and Cameron's father, I mean it's a complicated story, but I'll get to the point. My son is a good man and the fact that he didn't have sex with you yet says a lot so if you begin to freak out. He'll know what to do and he won't force you to do anything that you're not comfortable with. But it's a mind thing, for one try not to think about that night at all but if it do cross your mind please remind yourself that this isn't the man that raped you but that he's the man that loved you pass your rape. Once you get that in your head the both of you will be just fine.

"Thank you so much Miss Candace, I said to her while hugging her tightly.

"No problem and Nyla please call me mom; you are about to marry my son in less than two hours.

"Okay thanks mom."

"Anytime daughter, now let's get you down this aisle," she stated.

It was almost time for me to walk down the aisle and my stomach was doing backflips. The girls were dressed, and everyone looked beautiful. My makeup was flawless thanks to my best friend. The only thing I had to do was put on my dress and it was time. I haven't seen Zaire since last night and I only spoke to him once today. After talking to Zaire, I knew how my panties got around my ankles, I was showing my ass last night especially since I don't remember it. Tasha and Ariel helped me put my dress on and when I looked in the mirror, I couldn't believe how beautiful I looked.

"Hey sis are you ready?" Brandon asked but he stopped talking and just stared at me with his mouth wide open. Nyla you looking amazing, I can't believe you're getting married. Mom and dad would be so proud right now," Brandon stated with tears in his eyes causing me to tear up.

"Thank you, Brandon, but they would be prouder of you, you are the one that made me the woman I am today.

"I have something for you, you're supposed to have something old, something new, something borrowed and something blue. Well I have the something old that happens to be blue. These belonged to mom she wore these when she married dad. I had them redone for your special day. I started crying so hard as Brandon placed the blue pearl necklace around my neck.

"Aight with all this crying I'm gonna have to do your makeup over and then you'll be late to your wedding, Tasha said causing me to snap out of it. We all fixed ourselves up and took a few pics and I took some selfies. Mom Candace said a prayer before her and her sister walked out to be seated being escorted by Cameron who looked damn good, I couldn't wait to see my man. It was now my turn to walk out. I placed my arm inside of Brandon's arm and started walking out.

When the door open the few guest that was there stood up and "Every Time I Close My Eyes by Babyface," started playing. That was one of mine and Zaire's favorite songs, so we knew this was the song for us. But as I got further down the Aisle, I almost had a heart attack when I realized that it wasn't just the song playing but Babyface himself was standing next to Zaire singing me down the aisle. The tears fell freely down my face and I looked over at Tasha and Ariel and they were crying just as hard. I hoped my makeup wasn't looking crazy but the way I was crying I'm sure that I messed my face up. Zaire started walking towards me and Brandon and I was confused because that's not how it went. When he got to me and Brandon, he just stood there looking at me and that's when I realized that he was also crying.

"I'm sorry Brandon but this aisle is too long, and I couldn't wait for her to get to me, so I came to get my bride." Everyone was clapping and screaming out stuff. Zaire was looking super good right now.

Zaire was rocking a custom made royal blue custom-made tux with a white shirt a royal blue bowtie. The blue looked good on Zaire's perfectly light skin not to mention it complimented his sexy ass grey eyes. When we finally made it down the aisle Brandon gave me away and just like that I was married. I cried the entire ceremony, but it was beautiful and worth every tear. It was now time to take pictures before we had our little get together but all I was worried about was the honeymoon.

Chapter Twenty-Four

Zaire

I couldn't believe that I was now a married man. When I saw Nyla walking down the aisle looking as good as she did, she made, we wanna hurry up and make her my wife, so I went and got her. I loved Nyla with every fiber in my body and I was glad that I met Nyla. After taking pictures Nyla and I, both changed into some a little more comfortable, yet we was still fly. I had no intentions on being at this party for long I had big plans for my wife tonight and tomorrow and maybe for the rest of the trip with the way I was feeling. After we were changed, we met back up to be officially introduced.

Introducing for the first time Mr. Zaire and Nyla Price," Cameron stated and me and Nyla walked in but of course I was being extra and ended up picking my wife up to carry her in. The family ate that shit up. After we ate, my wife and I had our first dance even though, I think we did more kissing then we did dancing but that was fine with me. I danced with my mom and Nyla danced with

Brandon for the father and daughter dance. I fucked with Brandon because I loved the way he stepped up to the plate and raised his sisters even though he was still young himself.

So, Mrs. Price are you ready to get out of here and go make love all night long, I whispered in my wife's ear.

"Absolutely Mr. Price," she replied. With that I made an announcement that we were about to be out. We made our way around the room to say our goodbyes to everyone before we made our exit.

As soon as we got to the room, we started going at it like to teenagers in love. I wasted no time ripping Nyla out that dress and begin kissing and sucking on every part of her body. The way Nyla was into it I would have never thought for a moment that she was a virgin. But I knew I still had to take my time with her. Her moans had me brick hard and I was ready to feel her insides. I passionately kissed Nyla like I've never kissed anyone before making my way to her perfect sized breast. I placed her nipple in my mouth and gently sucked on both of her nipples.

"Mmm baby, this feels so good," Nyla cooed. Her chocolate body was everything and I couldn't wait to taste the chocolate in between her thighs. I licked every part of Nyla's, body until I reached her bare glistening inner folds in between her thighs. I slowly licked and sucked on Nyla's clitoris while gently rubbing on a hard nipple.

Nyla started gyrating her hips as I sucked and licked on her pearl. I knew she was close to cumming by the way she was acting. I started licking and sucking a little faster and just as I thought Nyla's nectar started to fill my mouth. "Oh God Zaire, I'm cumming!" Nyla moaned loudly yet sexy. I climbed on top of Nyla ready to insert my thickness inside of my wife.

"Are you ready?" I asked Nyla and she nodded her head yes. I gently entered Nyla's Wetness and she tensed up. I cupped her chin and looked her in her eyes. "Do you want me to stop?"

"No keep going just please don't hurt me you know I'm a virgin, she said with tears in her eyes and I looked down at her oddly because her words triggered me and had me tripping. She opened her eyes with concern.

"Is everything okay?"

"Everything is perfect," I lied. The truth was I was forced to rape a woman years ago and I'm not proud, but her words had taken me back to that night. I continued to slowly stroke in and out of Nyla's wetness and it was so tight and wet, but it also felt familiar, I was really tripping but kept going. I kissed Nyla I couldn't afford to mess this up.

"Ahh please be gentle," Nyla said with tears in her eyes and that was the moment I realized that my wife was the woman I raped!

To be continued……

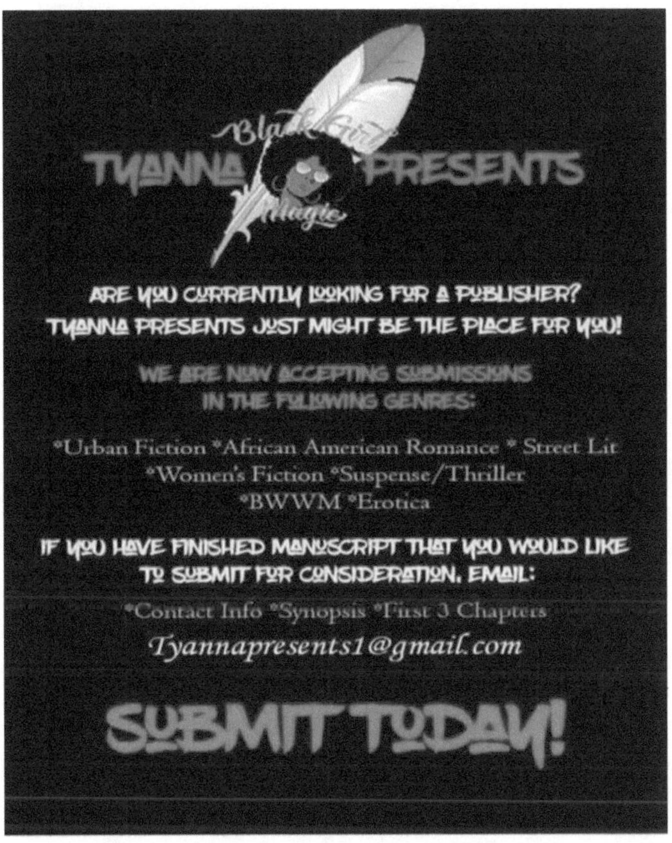

Black Girl Magic
TYANNA PRESENTS
ARE YOU CURRENTLY LOOKING FOR A PUBLISHER?
TYANNA PRESENTS JUST MIGHT BE THE PLACE FOR YOU!
WE ARE NOW ACCEPTING SUBMISSIONS
IN THE FOLLOWING GENRES:
*Urban Fiction *African American Romance * Street Lit
*Women's Fiction *Suspense/Thriller
*BWWM *Erotica
IF YOU HAVE FINISHED MANUSCRIPT THAT YOU WOULD LIKE
TO SUBMIT FOR CONSIDERATION, EMAIL:
*Contact Info *Synopsis *First 3 Chapters
Tyannapresents1@gmail.com
SUBMIT TODAY!